Neither God nor Devil

RETHINKING OUR PERCEPTION OF WOLVES

Eva-Lena Rehnmark

Pomegranate

SAN FRANCISCO

Published by Pomegranate Communications, Inc.
Box 6099, Rohnert Park, California 94927
www.pomegranate.com

Pomegranate Europe Ltd.
Fullbridge House, Fullbridge
Maldon, Essex CM9 4LE, England

Pomegranate Catalog No. A549

Library of Congress Cataloging-in-Publication Data

Rehnmark, Eva-Lena, 1973–
    Neither God nor devil : rethinking our perception of wolves / Eva-Lena Rehnmark.
        p. cm.
    Includes bibliographical references (p.)
    ISBN 0-7649-1338-7 (hb)
    1. Wolves. 2. Wolves—Folklore. 3. Human-animal relationships. I. Title.

QL737.C22 R43 2000
599.773—dc21
                                            00-027428

Cover and interior design by Wind Design, Mill Valley, California

PRINTED IN CHINA

09 08 07 06 05 04 03 02 01 00   10 9 8 7 6 5 4 3 2 1

Contents

Preface...iv

Acknowledgments vi

I. The Nature of Wolves 2

The Life of the Wolf......................................4

Canis Lupus, Canis Rufus, Canis Simensis 12

Recognizing Wolves 18

Captive Wolves 20

Wolf Society 22

Territory 26

Survival 28

Play 30

Vocalizations 32

Body Language 38

Passion..40

The Hunter..42

Wolves and Other Animals............................50

Wolves in Motion 54

Notes 55

II. Wolves of Myth.........................56

The Prehistoric Relationship.........................58

Fertility 60

Pathfinder and Teacher 62

The Wolf and the Viking...............................64

Wolf Clans 66

Masters of the Wolf 70

The Sacred Wolf...72

Lukos and *Luke* 74

Lycaon 75

Coursing through the Skies 76

Wolves and Death 78

Witches and Devils 80

Time 82

Storm and Wind...83

Opener of the Ways 84

Wolf Outlaw 86

Werewolf...88

The Wolf and the Lamb 90

Saints and Wolves 92

Science, Religion, and Magic 94

Wolves' Dark Ages..96

Notes 97

III. A Chronology of Wolves and Humans.............................98

Origins 101

Changing Times 103

Domestic Livestock and Depredation 104

The New World..109

Westward Exploration and Expansion 110

Fearing Wolves 112

Wolf Management 115

Wolves as Outlaws..116

Intolerance Toward Wolves...........................118

Changing Perceptions...................................120

Red Wolf Recovery.......................................122

Legal Battles 124

Defending Wolves 127

Surviving 128

Notes 130

Bibliography 132

Index 134

Preface

I have spent countless inspired hours with captive wolves, watching them pace back and forth behind a fence. I have drawn, painted, and sculpted them in an effort to record their intense gaze and incredible presence. In this time I have seen others approach the caged wolf; commonly they do so with spite, fear and, above all, prejudice. Nothing I have experienced while in the presence of wolves remotely justifies the fear that humans have for this animal. I even question whether wolves as I know them are the same creatures that the majority of humans despise so deeply that they have sought to eliminate the wolf from existence.

A belief that our impression of the wolf was once predominantly positive inspired my research into the history of wolves and humans. I sought to understand where this hatred came from and why our relationship with wolves had degenerated to its current sad state. What could have inspired hatred so strong that coexisting with the wolf has been considered impossible?

In order to gain insight on our ancestors' perception of wolves, I sought out ancient paintings, carvings, legends, and myths. I found artwork and mythology in which the wolf plays an important, influential, and positive role. Carved on bones and painted in caves, wolves appeared early in the birth of art; the famous Sorcerer of Trois Frères (from the Trois Frères cave at Ariège, France, dated to c. 13,000–11,000 B.C.), a painting of an antlered, lion-legged man/beast, is endowed with a wolf's tail. Ancient shamans such as this sorcerer took the form of a wolf in order to gain access to the animal's immense power. Many cultures believed that the wolf was a magical animal that could connect humans to the supernatural world. It was considered a manifestation of these beliefs that

wolves ate human corpses; the animals were thought to serve as vessels to carry the dead to the afterlife.

The wolf was not only divine, he was also our teacher. Traveling farther than humans could have dreamt possible, wolves were said to collect knowledge from distant corners of the earth. One area in which the wolf had superior knowledge was in hunting; numerous ancient tales tell of wolves that taught lessons to human hunters. These tales indicate that the techniques and cooperation employed by wolves in the hunt were imitated by humans. Wolves were also said to be the animal most similar to humans; some societies even claimed descent from the wolf. It is true that humans and wolves lived in much the same way, killing the same prey, scavenging from one another's kills, fasting when food was scarce and gorging in times of plenty. We lived in tightly knit family groups, as did the wolf, and some cultures even called the wolf their brother and built societies (wolf clans) in the animals' honor.

A drastic shift in attitude came with the adoption of a pastoral lifestyle. People who owned domestic stock saw the wolf as a threat. Though the wolf continued to be a totem animal, a teacher, and a fertility god, gradually its image darkened. Humans saw characteristics in the wolf that they had once shared, but which they no longer understood. A wolf gorging on prey was seen as a glutton, wolves killing prey were thought to do so with malice, and a wolf that was wary of man was thought to display cowardice. The age of the nomadic hunter-gatherer culture had passed, and with its passing our ability to relate to the wolf and its ways faded.

To further darken our perception of the wolf, at the birth of Christianity those promoting the new religion molded wolf gods and animistic beliefs into symbolism that supported the teachings of Christianity. This tactic was meant to discredit old teachings as well as to make the new beliefs more accessible by converting old deities to new demons. Thus, in Christian writings, the wolf was given the role of a devil that obstructed progress in a civilized and peaceful world. This symbol of the wolf threatening the lamb, which translates to "heathens threatening Christians," was convenient and convincing. The appropriation of wolf symbolism continued to evolve along these lines until the wolf represented the worst (i.e., the most primitive) attributes of humans. The wolf of myth became based on the flaws of man.

Myths of werewolves are a strong illustration of the mythical connection between wolves and the instinct-driven, baser part of man. Stories of cruel wolves that lurked in the forest waiting to violate the innocent taught women and children fear, keeping them at home: safe in the oppressive grip of fathers and husbands. The forest that was once familiar became terrifying, and in the wolf's very howl civilized humans found a blood-curdling reminder of the wilderness that surrounded them. We have been taught to fear the wolf of legend and myth, and this animal of our own creation has become so powerful and convincing that, in the minds of many, its image has become inseparable from the real wolf.

Even while studying the natural history of wolves, our own intuition can cloud our perceptions. An act by a wolf may be malicious according to human morals, but to wolves, it is an act necessary for pack survival. Humans are all too eager to categorize. Thus we face not only the difficulties of escaping the baggage of our ancestors and their mythology, but also the baggage of our species. The most open-minded scientist can unknowingly interpret data in a way that follows human beliefs. To exemplify this concept: alpha male wolves were traditionally considered the most active in the hunt. This belief is changing; female alpha animals are now recognized to be as important in the hunt as males, if not more so.

My objective is to represent a view of the wolf that is as full and three-dimensional as possible. My interest lies not only in understanding the wolf through science, but also in the perception of wolves that is inspired by passion and emotion. Although I am aware that collecting and interpreting scientific data is the way we can learn about the wolf with the least prejudice, I believe that an enormous amount of knowledge can be gained from studying the wolf's representation in literature, mythology, and art. Thus the first and second sections of this book are an overview of the wolf's natural history and of its history in mythology and art. The third section chronicles the effects humans have had on wolves and how we have endangered the wolf's very existence. This book is an account of the wolf as perceived and created by the human mind. To further that concept, it contains no photographs but is illustrated by drawings and paintings, my own interpretations of wolves.

What I hope for the wolf is that it will be seen as neither as god nor devil, but rather for what it is: an animal living peacefully in its own way, according to the nature of wolves.

Eva-Lena Rehnmark
San Francisco
January 2000

Acknowledgments

First I would like to thank my extraordinary parents for their decades of generous support and understanding. *Utan er skulle jag vara en fågel utan vingar.*

Thank you, Nina Fascione, for reading through early drafts of the work and checking it for accuracy. Thank you, Chantal Iyer, for translations, and Cornelia Hutt, for your enthusiasm and energy.

To the experts from around the world who responded to my requests for information—Jennifer Gilbreath in North Carolina, Luigi Boitani in Italy, Claudio Sillero in England/Ethiopia, Yadvendradev Jhala in India, Vadim Sidorovich in Belarus, Volodymyr Domashlinets in Ukraine, and especially Yorgos Iliopoulos in Greece—I extend my warm gratitude. What I found most stirring in my contact with wolf researchers was to see the wonder they express for the animals—in some cases after forty years of research.

I would also like to recognize the following libraries, which supplied the information for which I was so hungry: New York, San Francisco, Syracuse, and Marin County public libraries, and the U.C. Berkeley, Cornell, and Stanford university libraries.

I am deeply indebted to these authors: Bruce Hampton, Barry Lopez, David Mech, and John and Mary Theberge. Your books inspired me.

Thanks to Katie Burke and James Donnelly at Pomegranate for providing the means to share my fascination with wolves, and to designer Winslow Colwell.

And my heartfelt gratitude goes to Robert Stewart. You helped me see my own vision more clearly. You helped me to hold the balance between my heart and mind. You encouraged me when I was sure I could go no further.

Neither God nor Devil

The Nature of Wolves

Only once have I heard wolves howl in my presence.
The sound resonated deep within my chest,
not only for its penetrating pitch but also for the way
it touched my soul and evoked a reaction too profound
to be fueled by my own experience.

Existing literature, myth, and legend indicate that many others have had this same intense reaction to the wolf's howl. Some interpret it as awe, others as fear. I believe that the wolf's howl strikes a chord in our collective consciousness, serving as a reminder of an ancient lifestyle in which we were intimately connected to the natural world. How else can we explain why a simple vocalization touches us in a way that is not justified by our personal history with the animal?

For wolves, the sound that has fascinated us for thousands of years is a rich form of communication. In order to understand howling and other wolf traits, scientists study the species, analyze their findings, and draw conclusions about the animal's behavior. However, scientific findings can serve only as a starting point in fully understanding an animal. Hard facts are a limited means of understanding complex animals. Wolves, especially, are subtle and varied creatures, and there are few behavioral elements that are always true for all wolves. Therefore, it seems appropriate to keep one's idea of wolves undefined to some extent. With that in mind, the following is a description of how wolves commonly behave—a guideline rather than the ultimate truth about wolves.

A curious or stalking wolf will walk with its head lowered, staring intently with both eyes and ears focused on the object of interest. Sometimes a wolf will move its head from side to side, creating false motion that helps it to see.

The Life of the Wolf

From birth, wolves think and act independently. Although it may strike us as odd to regard wild animals as individuals, each wolf behaves distinctly enough to differentiate itself from other pack members. Some wolves, for example, are nervous or high-strung; others are confident and relaxed. One wolf may be prone to initiate play while another might behave aggressively; still another wolf may consistently retreat when threatened. Some wolves prefer solitude much of the time, though they still remain within the pack. Some are especially accomplished hunters, while others consistently stay with the pups and care for them. These individual temperaments help each wolf serve a particular role in the pack. In one pack of five wolves and pups, researchers discovered through genetic testing and by mapping the wolves' movements that the father spent the least amount of time with the pups. Instead he spent much of his time patrolling borders and going on solitary hunting forays. On the other hand, an unrelated male spent a great deal of time with the alpha male's offspring and rarely ventured far from them.[1]

MATING: Dominance rites are more pronounced just before mating season. In January and February, the alpha pair usually mates, though sometimes the alpha female will choose a lower-ranking mate. Like the alpha male, the female will prevent lower-ranking individuals of her sex from mating. Sometimes she will even intimidate other females to the point of preventing their estrus. After mating occurs, the pack may split up into smaller hunting groups for the duration of the winter months, when prey can be scarce.

DENNING: Toward the end of her nine-week gestation, the alpha female locates and digs the den. Finding an appropriate den site is a complex decision, since the pack needs to stay in the chosen location for six to eight weeks, or until the pups are old enough to be moved. If a den site is chosen in an area of little prey, the pack may have to leave the area early, jeopardizing the pups' survival. When the alpha female has found the site, she digs a den with an entrance tunnel of six to twelve feet and a diameter of fifteen to twenty-five inches, ending in a birthing chamber. Sometimes a cave, a hollow log, or an old fox den is selected and enlarged to the appropriate size. Wolves are not tolerant of intense animal or human activity near their dens and when disturbed have been known to abandon the den or move the pups prematurely.

Pups look little like wolves at this early stage: they have dark fur, their muzzles are short, their eyes have not opened, and their ears are still close to their heads.

BIRTH: In March or April, a litter of four to six puppies (with a known maximum of fourteen) is born deaf and blind, weighing about one pound each. By this time the pack is together again and they bring food to the mother. This enables her to stay with the pups to keep them warm. At this age pups only have downy underfur, and cannot yet regulate their own body heat. Sometimes other females will also lactate, providing extra nourishment for the pups or serving as backups for the birth mother. The pups gain an average of three pounds per week.

The bond between parents and pups is very strong. In the following account from Adolph Murie's *The Wolves of Mt. McKinley*, a biologist removed a one-week-old pup from its den in May. Three months later, while chained outside a cabin, "the wolf pup was heard whining softly. On looking out I saw the black female only a few yards from the pup. The following evening . . . I heard the pup whining again and saw the black female with it. She traveled slowly and reluctantly up the slope, looking back repeatedly. The pup tried to follow and when it reached the end of the chain, kept jumping forward to be away."[2]

Canis simensis

A similar link between pack members and a pup was recorded in R. D. Lawrence's *In Praise of Wolves*: A captive pack's caretaker removed a sick pup to raise it indoors. Delaying its normal activities, the pack searched and mourned for the lost wolf pup. After several weeks the pup was returned to the enclosure, causing an unusual commotion among the wolves. The adult wolves "began whining and dancing, climbing over one another in their excitement. . . ." The pup was placed on the ground "and actually ran toward his mother. . . . The wolves crowded around him at first, intimidating him, but when the pup realized he could play-fight with each one in turn with complete impunity, and that every wolf allowed him to do pretty much as he liked, his happiness was complete."[3]

At the age of three weeks, pups can see and hear; they venture more frequently from the safety of the den.

The entire pack will participate in raising the pups by providing food for both the lactating mother and the pups. The pack also shares in the responsibilities of discipline, caretaking, and playing with the pups. Once the pups are out of the den, pack members are extraordinarily patient with them, acting as jungle gyms for the rambunctious pups, which bite, chew, wrestle, pounce on, tackle, and generally harass the adults. If a wolf pup is disrespectful and goes too far in its play, an adult will pin it to the ground for a moment by its muzzle, and sometimes growl as a warning.

TWO WEEKS: Pups are able to see.

THREE WEEKS: At this age pups can hear and they emerge from the den active and playful. They pounce on each other, present sticks and pieces of fur to each other as gifts, and prance about gripping trophies in their mouths (feathers, bones, sticks, caribou skin). One pup was observed repeatedly tossing a flattened, dried-up frog into the air and catching it. Such play continues throughout the wolf's life.

Another social element that starts early is the wolf hierarchy system. From an early age the pups have their own version of the pack social structure, featuring alpha, beta, and lower-ranking individuals. The

Though this may just be a moment of interrupted play, it is likely that the wolf pup standing over the other is displaying her dominance.

dominant pup fights and wrestles the other pups to maintain his position. The hierarchy generally shifts a great deal until, between four and seven weeks of age, one wolf has established clear dominance in a more serious fight.

FOUR TO FIVE WEEKS: By now the pups are weaned from their mother's milk and are ready to eat meat. Adults travel several miles from the kill to the den carrying partially digested food in their stomachs, and regurgitate a portion when the pups lick or nip underneath their muzzles.

EIGHT WEEKS: At this age the pups are moved to a rendezvous site close to new hunting grounds. Essentially a meeting spot for the wolves that roam their territory searching for prey, the rendezvous sites are where the pack will rest, play, and socialize. The pups remain at the site alone or with an adult during these warmer months, when the hunters commonly leave at night and return in the morning. Exploring,

running, jumping, playing, climbing, and mouthing everything in sight, the pups are entertained until the hunting adults return with food. The rendezvous site consists of systems of trails, areas of play indicated by trampled grass, and a number of beds—like dogs, wolves turn and scrape at their bedding sites to make them more comfortable. After a few weeks the wolves move on to the next site (sometimes up to five miles away). By moving from site to site, they are able to cover much of the hunting ground in their territory.

FIVE TO SEVEN MONTHS: As soon as the pups can walk they will pounce on mice and chase rabbits, but normally they will not catch anything larger until late fall, when they will learn how to tackle large-hoofed prey.

SEVEN TO EIGHT MONTHS: By fall prey is generally abundant, and pups begin to travel with the adults, learning how to hunt large game with the pack. Wolf adults and pups howl more than usual in late summer and fall.

TWENTY-TWO MONTHS: At this age wolves are able to breed (though they rarely do so until they are four years old), and their position of dominance in the pack is clarified.

DISPERSAL: At any time in its adult life a wolf might decide or be forced to leave the pack; it can comfortably travel more than twenty miles a day to find a pack and/or its own territory. For example, two female littermates might disperse together and join an unrelated male on his territory. The farthest known dispersal was 687 miles by a wolf in Sweden. It is much more dangerous to be a disperser wolf than a pack member. The death rate for these wolves is almost as high as that of pups, which can be more than 50 percent.

OLD AGE: Although older wolves are physically unable to contribute as much as younger wolves, they are still important members of the pack. Older wolves offer vital knowledge gained from years of experience, such as where to find prey or where to den. They are usually well cared for by their pack members. Old alpha wolves that can no longer defend their status are replaced and sometimes exiled from the pack. When older wolves are lost due to natural or human causes, their loss can be traumatic enough to split the pack.

Although pups' eyes open at twelve to fifteen days old, they are unable to distinguish forms until weeks later.

When a pup mouths an adult wolf's muzzle, it is a signal for the adult wolf to regurgitate food. This behavior continues throughout a wolf's life as a sign of submission.

Wolves can be very tender toward one another.

Death

NATURAL CAUSES: The dangers in the wild are many. Wolves die from starvation (mainly pups) or are killed by disease, by parasites, or by other wolves defending their territories. Injury inflicted by prey is another, less common cause of death. In eleven years only two wolves in John Theberge's study in Algonquin National Park (Canada) died from prey-inflicted wounds. Fifty-six out of 110 wolves autopsied in the Tanama River region of Alaska were found to have survived traumatic injuries—skull, leg, and rib fractures that had partially or completely healed.[4] For example, one of the collared Algonquin Park wolves starved to death after surviving five broken ribs (one of which had not healed), a broken leg (which had fused crookedly), and a stick lodged between its upper carnassial teeth. The stick had been in place so long that the wolf's gums had adjusted to the foreign object.

HUMAN CAUSES: Wolves living in close proximity to humans are more likely to be killed by snare, gunshot, poison, or run-ins with cars than by any natural cause. Because so many people still believe in the old saying "the only good wolf is a dead one," scientists studying wolves often find their efforts both intentionally and unintentionally thwarted. Biologists discovered that radio-collared wolves were killed all around the borders of Algonquin Park. However, because their collars were smashed the number of wolves lost was unknown. In the same study 55 percent of the still-collared wolves were found dead in one year, all but one by human causes.[5] Even pet wolves that escape from their enclosures are often shot within twenty-four hours. In most cases those who make a habit of killing wolves do not know much about the animal; they do not consider that the wolf belongs to a family in which it has a particular role. In areas where this kind of killing is rampant, the loss of pack members can be severely damaging to the pack's social structure.

MOURNING: Wolves have deep social ties. When a member of the pack has died, wolves are believed to mourn its death. When a farmer killed one pack's alpha female, a wolf in the pack repeatedly howled "long, forlorn notes breaking downward in melancholy intervals."[6] Researchers and captive wolf caretakers have noted this same type of howl upon the death or injury of pack members. In some cases wolves stay near dead or dying pack members for a few days; in areas set up with traps and snares this sort of dedication has proven tragic. Normal pack behavior will often cease: for days or weeks wolves may not play or even hunt.

Sometimes deaths cause a pack to split, producing fugitive wolves of a once-close family. Territory once rich with pack structure and wolf activity becomes an area of unsettled wolves. Searching for a mate or a pack to join, such wolves can form temporary alliances. These wolves, whether old or young, lose the safety and comfort of the pack and become dispersers whose lives are more risky and difficult.

One captive wolf was seen taking a dead pup out of the den and burying its body at the edge of the enclosure. There is no known reason for this sort of activity. The rest of the pack did not disturb the grave, though they often dug up old bones from other animals.[7]

GRAY WOLF (*Canis lupus*)

Ecological status: vulnerable

Crepuscular (most active during dawn and dusk), though wolves in the least populated areas seem to prefer to hunt during daylight hours.

Height: 2.5 feet at the shoulder (up to 3 feet)

Length, nose to tail tip: 5 to 5.5 feet long (up to 6.5 feet)

Weight: 50 to 100 pounds. (largest wolf on record was 170 pounds.)

Canine teeth: 1 to 1.25 inches long

Pack size: 6 to 10 (up to 30 in northern regions)

Litter: 4 to 6 pups (known maximum 14 pups)

Territory: 20 to 150 square miles (200 to 1,000 far north; known maximum of 5,000 square miles)

Traveling speed: 5 miles per hour, 10 to 25 miles per day

Maximum speed: 40 miles per hour

Life expectancy: 8 years average; some live 13 years or more (in areas of heavy exploitation by humans, wolves live an average of 5-6 years)

Paw print size: typically 4.5 to 5.5 inches long, but can reach 6 inches

Habitat: forests, taiga, tundra, deserts, plains, and mountains

Canis Lupus

Subspecies of Canis Lupus

IN NORTH AMERICA:

- 🐾 **Arctic Wolf**
  (*Canis lupus arctos*),
  historical range: Melville
  and Ellesmere Islands
- 🐾 **Mexican Wolf**
  (*Canis lupus baileyi*),
  historical range: foothills and
  mountains of central Mexico,
  southeastern Arizona, southern
  New Mexico, and southwestern
  Texas. *Canis lupus baileyi* has
  been extinct in the wild since
  1980, only existing in captive
  breeding programs and in a
  small reintroduced "nonessential, experimental" population
  in the wild (see page 123).
  This subspecies of the gray
  wolf is believed to be the rarest
  mammal in North America.
- 🐾 **Mackenzie Valley Wolf**
  (*Canis lupus occidentalis*), historical range: Alaska, western
  Canada

C. l. arctos

C. l. Arabs

- 🐾 **Eastern Timber Wolf**
  (*Canis lupus lycaon*), historical
  range: southeastern Canada to
  New England. Current studies
  indicate that *Canis lupus lycaon*
  may be the same species as *Canis
  rufus* (see page 16).[8]
- 🐾 **Great Plains or Buffalo Wolf**
  (*Canis lupus nubilus*), historical
  range: North American Plains.
  Canis lupus nubilus was once
  thought to be extinct, but now
  some scientists speculate that
  this wolf's descendants live in
  Minnesota, Wisconsin, and
  Michigan.

- **Common Wolf**
  (*Canis lupus lupus*), historical range:
  Europe, forested Russia
- **Tundra Wolf**
  (*Canis lupus albus*), historical range:
  northern Russia, northern
  Scandinavia
- **Wolf of Southern Arabia**
  (*Canis lupus Arabs*), historical range:
  Saudi Arabia, Israel
- **Steppe Wolf**
  (*Canis lupus campestris*), historical
  range: Central Asia
- **Ezo Wolf of Hokkaido**
  (*Canis lupus hattai*), historical range:
  Japan (extinct)
- **Wolf of Honshu**
  (*Canis lupus hodophiliax*),
  historical range: Japan (extinct)
- **Tibetan Wolf**
  (*Canis lupus laniger*), historical range:
  Mongolia, Tibet, China
- **Wolf of India and Iraq**
  (*Canis lupus pallipes*), historical
  range: India, Iraq, Israel, Turkey,
  and Saudi Arabia
- **Domestic Dog**
  (*Canis lupus familiaris*), range:
  nearly every place where humans
  exist. See caption, page 19.

C. l. lupus

It was once believed that there were thirty-two subspecies of wolves, but modern scientists maintain that only twelve genetically distinct subspecies of wolves currently inhabit the world. This contrast is due less to extinction than to the wide variation in peltage and size within what are now viewed as the same subspecies. Scientists have still not determined the number and range of these subspecies; China is currently reclassifying its three indigenous subspecies into five.

*Canis lupus has historically had the greatest
natural range of any species other than man.*

RED WOLF (*Canis rufus*)

Ecological status: declared extinct in the wild in 1980; reintroduced by USFWS in 1987

Crepuscular (most active during dawn and dusk), tends to be more diurnal in winter

Height: 1.9 to 2.25 feet

Length, nose to tail tip: 4.6 to 5.4 feet

Weight: 42 to 84 pounds

Pack size: up to 11

Territory: 17 to 87 square miles

Habitat: coastal plains, forests, and farms of southeastern United States

Original range: eastern Canada to central Texas

Canis Rufus

Once thought to be a hybrid of gray wolves and coyotes, now scientists consider the red wolf a unique, primitive species of wolf. As proof, red wolf skulls dated at 1,500,000 years old have been discovered in Florida and other locations in the Southeastern US, indicating that canis rufus is an ancient and distinct species. Red wolves and the wolves studied in Algonquin Park (Canada) are believed to be one and the same species, genetically distinct from *Canis lupus*.

Canis Simensis

Ethiopian wolves are unique in that most of their food comes from solitary foraging, though they do maintain close-knit packs, all members of which help to protect and feed the young. They display pack solidarity in ways similar to other wolves, with energetic, noisy greetings. However, *Canis simensis* females often mate with males from another pack (70 percent of the time in one study).[9] This practice is unique to this species of wolf and may be intended to increase genetic variation, since members of the pack are commonly related. Dispersal is rare since there is little suitable unoccupied territory.

Although *Canis simensis* was believed to belong to the jackal family, DNA tests indicate that the animal is indeed a wolf. It is theorized that the Ethiopian wolf is an evolutionary relic of a red wolflike animal that crossed the Bering land bridge from North America into Eurasia and onward to Africa between six and eight hundred thousand years ago. Ethiopian wolves adapted to the Afro-alpine plateaus by preying upon rodents, of which there are such high densities that they compete with the richness of the ungulate biomass in the African savannah.

ETHIOPIAN WOLF (*Canis simensis*)
Ecological status: the most critically endangered canid; fewer than five hundred remain in a dozen isolated mountain ranges in Ethiopia. A small captive breeding population has been established to release in the wild if necessary.
Diurnal (active during the day), but in areas with close proximity to humans, wolves are increasingly active at night.
Height: 1.25 to 1.33 feet
Length: 3.4 to 4.3 feet
Weight: 20 to 40 pounds
Territory: 4 square miles
Habitat: highlands of Ethiopia at altitudes up to 14,100 feet
Pack size: up to 13 adult wolves, plus the year's litter (typically 6 pups)

Captive Wolves

People seeking an unusual pet may consider buying a wolf or wolf-dog hybrid. This is a very serious decision to make: properly caring for this animal consumes an extraordinary amount of time and energy. Although it is possible to rear a wolf successfully, many people who decide to undertake such a commitment never do it again. In their books, David Mech, Barry Lopez, and Lois Crisler have all made apologies to the wolves they kept. There is plenty of literature available about keeping wolves, and it is vital to know as much about the subject as possible before making the decision (see bibliography, p. 133).

Wolf-dog hybrids are an odd mix and can be very dangerous. There is no way to know which characteristics the animal will inherit. The wolf-dog could gain the appearance of a normal dog paired with a wolf's instinct, which can make him difficult to train. Wolf puppies which are intended to be kept as pets should be hand-reared from no later than twenty-one days old. After that they are more difficult to manage and may be indifferent toward humans. A dedicated socialization period with hours of daily handling is necessary for captive wolf pups to grow up friendly and affectionate. Past the age of three months even hand-reared pups naturally become cautious or fearful of strangers. Born with instincts and needs that cannot be fulfilled in a captive environment, wolves and wolf-dogs do not fit comfortably into a household the same way a domestic dog does. Unfortunately, most of the hybrids that people bring home end up being put to sleep by owners that love them dearly but have to choose between owning a wolf or having a normal life.

To keep a captive wolf, one must enclose a highly social animal that prefers to live in a pack and is built to travel twenty or more miles each day. David Mech writes of his wolf Lightning that after she escaped "she was still tame and gentle with me, but she had finally gotten a taste of what it was like to act as her heritage had dictated, to be wild and free. As I watched Lightning straining desperately at her chain, pacing, whining, and jumping frantically, I suddenly realized how very wrong it is to try to tame a wolf."[10]

Those who are able to raise wolves or hybrids with some degree of success often find that prejudice and hatred toward wolves exists everywhere. Many have had their pets poisoned or shot by those who fear or hate wolves. Some wolves have even been shot while on a chain in their owners' backyards! Captive wolves can also add to the negative public opinion of wild wolves. With every headline of children mauled by wolf-hybrids that were poorly trained or played with too roughly, or pet wolves who didn't know how to react to a small child, people automatically associate such behavior with wild wolves. The resulting downward swing in the public opinion of wolves could greatly jeopardize recovery plans as well as natural repopulation.

CAPTIVE RESEARCH: To study wolves in captivity and relate findings to wolves in the wild is a practice fraught with risk. Wolves that live in a very limited space, are prevented from hunting or traveling, and are constantly in the company of other wolves or human visitors, will often exhibit extreme behavior. Among these behaviors are excessive social displays and violence, especially around food (whereas people observing them in the wild are surprised at how benign they are around a kill). Often one wolf in a captive pack will become a scapegoat, and will be constantly harassed by the other wolves. Because this wolf cannot escape—which would calm tensions in the pack—the situation can become progressively worse.

Captive wolves are only a spectre of their wild counterparts. Limits on behavior and movement allow few wolf characteristics to be fulfilled.

Wolf Society

A wolf pack consists of a group of wolves that are not necessarily related but live and hunt together, form bonds with each other, show stress when separated, and rejoice when reunited. The bonds formed between a mating pair can be so strong that these wolves are rarely more than one hundred meters apart. Each wolf pack has its own personality, so much so that people familiar with the pack can recognize its wolves from far away by observing the way they behave and interact with each other.

A wolf pack is held together by a strong system of social pressure and interdependence. When the pups are young the adult members of the pack feed them and will also eventually teach them how to hunt. When those adults grow older and their ability to catch prey deteriorates, the young wolves share their kills with them. The relationship between wolves within the pack structure is circular; every wolf serves as both a caretaker and a recipient. This scenario has also been observed with captive wolves: at the Chicago zoo a sixteen-year-old, arthritic wolf that rarely left the sleeping quarters was brought food by the other wolves.[11] Food is shared in a wolf pack even when not all of the pack members are involved in the hunt. Only in times of famine is more food reserved for the hunters.

The wolf in the upper-left-hand corner of this image is a beta pack member displaying his dominance to the lower-ranking wolf below him. The wolf to the right of the beta is the current alpha male. His ears are up and forward, displaying both attentiveness and confidence. The wolf to the alpha's right has her ears slightly back and her mouth in an open, submissive grin. The wolf lying down is the former alpha male.

23

The wolf to the left is the dominant individual and is pressing the other wolf's muzzle between her jaws in a display of her higher rank.

Social Order

A social hierarchy is formed within a wolf pack in order to ease tension and maintain harmony. This hierarchy begins when a pup is born and changes throughout the wolf's life.

Wolves constantly reaffirm their various positions in the pack using the body language and facial expressions of dominance or subordination. A threat is generally expressed by snarling, growling, and raising the tail and hackles in order to appear as large and as dangerous as possible. When threatened by a wolf with a lower rank, the dominant animal must defend his or her position with a threatening display. If neither wolf reverts to submissive behavior (tail tucked tight under its belly, ears flattened, sometimes rolling over on its back), a fight may occur. Though serious fights are uncommon they do happen, and some wolves will fight to the death to keep or improve their rank. Such serious fights are eerily silent and other pack members will often take sides

and get involved. Though aggression is used in maintaining rank, the predominant behavior in a wolf pack is friendly.

ALPHA: The wolves that command the greatest respect are the alpha males and females. Either one can be dominant, although usually the alpha female takes control before she gives birth. The alpha male and alpha female are usually the only pack members who are allowed to mate, although sometimes, especially in an area with plentiful prey, a second or even third female produces pups. The alpha must be a bright and strong wolf with the energy and traits required to acquire and maintain the highest rank.

Defining the position of alpha wolves is complicated. The leader seems to make decisions on his or her own, but can be swayed by the reaction of the pack. The leader is generally the most motivated pack member, deciding when to hunt, when to sleep, and when to awaken; the alpha often rises first and awakens the rest of the pack. The alpha leader shows initiative and ambition, and motivates the rest of the pack to follow.

BETA: Either a single wolf or a pair follows the alpha pair in rank. The beta wolf or wolves will often defend the alpha pair in its decisions.

OMEGA: As the lowest-ranking member, the omega wolf sometimes receives a great deal of abuse from the pack. Omegas can be banished, killed, starved, or generally harassed, though it is unknown how often these behaviors occur in the wild, since most observation of this behavior has occurred in captive packs. It is not clear why the omega is sometimes treated so poorly. There are many possible reasons: it may refuse to cooperate with rules of the pack, may steal food, may be sick, or may threaten the pack in some way.

In one captive pack a female refused to have any contact with three unfamiliar pups that were brought to stay with her and her mate. The alpha male accepted the pups while the female escaped to the far end of the enclosure. No longer a member of the pack, she was not allowed to feed with them or be involved in other pack activities such as play and howling sessions. When the lone female was tranquilized and inspected, the caretakers found that she had a cataract in her eye that made her partially blind. It is likely that her blindness made her fearful of the new animals that were released in the enclosure, preventing her from bonding with them.[12]

Wolf Justice

Wolf researchers have observed that packs function differently under different alpha wolves. Though other old wolves are usually treated kindly, it has been observed that if an alpha wolf treats pack members poorly, it is attacked and banished once it loses its position. The order in a wolf pack can change very quickly. The alpha may be challenged and beaten in a fight with another male, entirely overturning the pack structure. Such fights are rarely private quarrels; the whole pack will get involved. Serious wolf fights, however, are very rare; few conflicts go past a threat.

One type of appeasement behavior by submissive wolves is licking another wolf's muzzle.

Territory

Wolves occupy a territory whose size is determined by the area's prey density and the size of the pack. The alpha wolf or wolves will urinate frequently around the boundaries as well as the interior of the territory to ensure that the scent is always fresh. The scent serves as a sort of "smell map" of the territory; some scientists suggest that this marking helps the resident pack find its way around. Another purpose of scent marking is to clarify to other wolves that the territory is currently occupied and that trespassers risk attack by the resident pack. Meetings with wolves outside of the pack are generally hostile. More energy is expended on maintaining a larger territory and protecting it and the prey within it from other wolves and encroaching packs.

The borders of wolf territory are to some extent flexible. There are established buffer zones, a "no-man's-land" between territories that prevents accidental trespassing. In some cases researchers have found that wolf packs that share borders in certain areas are actually an enlarged extended family, and that is why they allow trespassing and sometimes even hunting. In other cases it seems that the pack decides whether it is worth the expenditure of energy to defend a large territory simply with the purpose of keeping all prey for itself. When the territory is small it may be worth the cost of aggressive defense in order to keep the prey. However, when wolves follow deer to winter feeding grounds, different packs can be concentrated in a relatively small area and rarely show territorial aggression. In the most extreme case two packs were even reported to have peacefully shared one kill. In situations where prey is abundant there is less need to display territorial aggression.

Wolves, like dogs, really seem to enjoy rolling in foul-smelling substances. It was once thought that wolves did so to camouflage their own scent from prey. Now scientists believe that they are either carrying the smell to other pack members or rubbing their own scent onto the odd-smelling object (such as rotten fish, perfume, or soap).

Survival

ADAPTABILITY: On Isle Royale, Michigan, wolves changed their behavior to adapt to unusually heavy snows. Because of the weather, both wolves and moose traveled shorelines and inland lakes more frequently, so there were more encounters between them. Wolves took advantage of this situation by hunting in larger packs (usually packs split into smaller hunting groups in winter) and were able to triple the number of moose that they killed. In a similar situation, Algonquin Park researchers discovered that wolves did not follow deer in their migration to a winter feeding ground; instead, they waited in ambush along deer trails. Such adaptations to changes in prey and environment are necessary for the wolves' survival.

INSULATION: Like many canids, wolves have a double layer of fur that helps keep them warm. The fluffy underfur, which is short and fine, grows thick for the cold seasons and is shed in the spring. The outer layer of fur is made up of guard hairs that repel water and wind, enabling the underfur to work as an insulator, trapping air warmed by the wolf's body heat. Arctic wolves have longer guard hairs and a thicker layer of underfur than other gray wolf subspecies, creating effective protection from the elements. A wolf can survive temperatures far below zero by digging a hole in the snow (or using some other wind block) to shelter itself from the wind and by curling up, covering its nose and mouth with its tail.

CLEANLINESS: Wolves generally go to great lengths to keep themselves clean and groomed. They take baths regularly, sometimes both before and after eating, to clean themselves of blood and dirt. In spring when they are shedding, they roll on the ground and rub up against rough surfaces to rid themselves of extra underfur. However, not all wolves are so particular. Photographer Jim Brandenburg and biologist David Mech named one of the arctic wolves they observed "Scruffy" because of the muddied tufts of shedding hair that hung all over his pelt. Another wolf from the same pack was blackened with mud in pursuit of a hare. Carrying the hare firmly in his jaws the wolf trotted to the nearest water. After cleaning himself, he shook his coat dry and finally began to eat.[13]

CACHE: Many wolves bury a cache of excess meat to eat later. While the pups are young, food is often cached close to the den so that the mother does not have to be far from the pups; otherwise the meat is usually cached close to the kill. When wolves dig up buried meat they shake it vigorously in their mouths to remove as much dirt as possible (unless the meat was cached in the snow). Often a wolf's cache is dug up and eaten by other animals.

Arctic wolves have both longer guard hairs and a thicker layer of underfur than other gray wolf subspecies, creating a dense protection from the elements.

Play

Wolves have been known to play together or alone for hours. A lone wolf was once seen tossing a piece of caribou hide into the air and catching it in his mouth. He was amused by this game for an entire hour. Pups and adults play the wolf equivalents of hide-and-seek, tag, and keep-away. They pounce on sleeping wolves, surprise each other by jumping unexpectedly from hiding places, and bring each other "gifts" and bits of food. Writer Lois Crisler's two wolves seemed to especially enjoy a particular game. One or both wolves would dig a hole and sniff at it excitedly as if there were a mouse there. Invariably one wolf was tempted to go to the other's hole.[14]

R. D. Lawrence observed eight wolves on a frozen lake in Canada that were

dashing about over the ice, at times bunching up, on other occasions spreading out over an area of some four hundred square feet . . . a definite game was in progress. Seven of the wolves were chasing a large individual, clearly the pack leader, each trying to make contact with him. The Alpha was dashing about wildly, at one moment running at full speed, at another coming to an abrupt, sliding stop that swiveled his hindquarters, much as an automobile skids around when braked abruptly on a slippery surface. The result of this maneuver was that the big wolf turned about, sliding sideways. This caused the pursuers to run right past him, all of them sliding also as they tried to stop in order to turn and continue the chase. Recovering his balance, the leader would then charge into the rearmost of his pursuers, hitting it with his chest and sending it rolling over and over, skidding helplessly on the snowy ice. When this happened, the seven chasers would bark shrilly, including the one that had been bowled over, as though registering their pleasure and amusement. Then the whole show began over again.[15]

31

Vocalizations

We recognize wolves more for their howl than for any other characteristic. Besides spotting a wolf's tracks, which requires a trained and attentive eye, hearing its howl is the simplest, and often the only, way for us to experience the animal in the wild. Since wolves have learned to fear and avoid humans, physically encountering the wolf in its habitat is extremely rare. Researchers who do not use telemetry devices can spend an entire lifetime in the field without seeing a wolf. Although a howl can be heard over an area of fifty square miles, this animal's other vocalizations (barks, whines, and growls) are not intended to carry long distances and are rarely heard.

This vocalization can also be invoked by human imitation. Surprisingly, wolves are more likely to respond to human howls than to recorded wolf howls. In summer and fall, wolves howl frequently and will respond to nearly anything, even fire alarms. Occasionally young wolves have responded to a researcher's imitation by bounding happily toward him or her; upon finding a human instead of a wolf, they have fled as quickly as they appeared. Although researchers express valid concerns that human howling may disrupt the wolf's normal activity, howling is one of very few ways we can communicate and interact with the otherwise elusive wolf.

Wolf pups begin howling as young as twenty-eight days old.

Alarm

Challenge

The complex language of the wolf is not fully understood, but we do know that communication is of utmost importance within a pack of wolves. There is a full range of vocalizations:

ALARM: Wolves use a muffled "woof" or short bark, sometimes accompanied by a howl, to express fear or surprise. This vocalization sends pups scrambling to the den. The louder bark can also be used with a howl, presumably to call pack members back to the den to protect pups from intruders.

CHALLENGE: Wolves can voice a threat with one or two barks followed by a drawn-out bark, and/or deeper barks sometimes followed by a growl. This vocalization is sometimes accompanied by the snapping of teeth. In this case the wolf's bark acts as a warning to the intruder or challenger that attack is imminent.

ATTENTION: Whimpers, whines, whistles, and squeaks are the vocalizations most often used in the pack. All of these vocalizations seem to be friendly calls for attention, stemming from a desire to play or to acquire food, care, or warmth. Wolves can also squeal in response to pain, terror, or fear.

AGGRESSION: The growl is a vocalization used to assert dominance, to threaten, or to challenge. Wolves will growl to warn pups to discontinue certain behaviors, or to defend food or possessions. When used as intimidation before an attack, growls can be accompanied by raised hackles, snapping teeth, or teeth bared in an open mouth (as opposed to the friendly or submissive tooth-baring "smile").

Purpose of Howling

Howling serves as a means of communication within the pack as well as a way to alert outside wolves of their presence. Wolves that approach the source of howl imitations are most likely seeking to rejoin their pack. When wolves become separated, howling is an effective way for the animals to locate and regain contact with one another. There is even a specific howl used when one wolf is separated from the pack. This particular howl, with a rising and falling crescendo, is also heard upon the death of a pack member.

In addition to collecting a scattered pack, this vocalization seems to bind the pack by strengthening social ties. The howl is a way for wolves to affirm and display their unity. When one animal initiates a howl, fellow pack members seek out contact with one another, displaying friendliness, tail wagging, and bright-eyed excitement. Researchers suggest that this ceremony exists to reinforce the pack structure and loyalty, which are vital to the wolf's existence.

Another purpose of the howl is to ensure that traveling wolves or neighboring packs are aware of the size, location, and solidarity of the resident wolf family. A pack is able to announce its numbers by howling in harmony. Because a large pack indicates strength, wolves adamantly avoid howling in unison. This practice is so effective that humans who hear howling in the wild often greatly overestimate the number of wolves. A small pack will not answer larger packs for fear of instigating territorial aggression. For the same reason, a lone wolf traveling through occupied territory will refrain from howling.

The wolf's howl, which connotes family and togetherness, is a fitting signature for the species.

Biologist Duward Allen called howling "the jubilation of wolves."

Body Language

The play bow—front legs to the ground and hind end in the air—is intended to initiate play.

With laid-back ears and a snapping, open-mouthed growl, this wolf clearly has aggressive intentions.

Wolves are capable of a great range of expressions. The ears, eyes, tail, and mouth are the main indicators of a wolf's mood. An aggressive or dominant wolf tries to make itself seem as large and threatening as possible, whereas a subordinate does the opposite. An aggressive mood is conveyed by a tail high and stiff, corners of the mouth pulled forward, and ears forward. A wolf signals submission by holding its tail low or

During mating season males will approach the ovulating female enthusiastically. They will paw at her, try to mount her, and generally vie for her attention. In this case the female is growling and unre- ceptive to the light-colored male. She may not be ready to mate. The dark male is displaying his dominance with a stiff-legged stance, erect ears and tail, and a growl.

This wolf is displaying his subordination with laid-back ears, lips pulled back into a "grin," and tail tucked tight to the belly.

between its legs, pulling back the corners of its mouth, and flattening its ears. Aggressive physical behavior is generally shown through a stiff body posture. Lunging or snapping at, shoving, pressing, pinning, standing over, slamming, or body-bashing another wolf is considered a challenge. Submissive physical behavior is generally expressed through a more flexible posture, including lowering the body or rolling over onto the back. Aggression tends to increase during breeding season. Wolves try to resolve a challenge through threats and intimidation rather than through fighting in order to avoid exertion and injury.

A signal of excitement in wolves, tail wagging can be a friendly or an aggressive gesture. Wagging the tail slowly and stiffly is a sign of dominance. Friendly greetings are accompanied by a loosely wagging tail.

These pups are not just playing; they are involved in a display of social hierarchy. The light-colored pup is showing her dominance over the other pup by pressing him to the ground with her body.

Passion

Humans pride themselves in being the only member of the animal kingdom that acts not only out of instinct but also out of passion. The truth is, we may not be alone in this respect. Scientists have traditionally set forth that animals react instinctively to their surroundings, always choosing the path that will result in the smallest amount of energy expenditure and the least chance of immediate harm. Theories like this make the colorful and fascinating behavior of wolves seem dull and mechanical. There is evidence to support the idea that wolves are much more than slaves to instinct. Consider the actions of a wolf pack that attacked grizzly bears when there was no immediate danger to the pack or the den:

Four grizzly bears initiated the attack by wandering too close to a den full of wolf pups. On the following day the pack of twelve hunting members sought out the bears, an animal that has been known to kill and eat wolves. There was no evidence of the threats usually made to avoid a fight; the wolf pack simply attacked the bears. Two of the yearling bears were killed. A young bear, a big sow, and most of the wolves were wounded. The attack was almost certainly made in an effort to defend the pups, but since there was no direct threat to the pups, it appears that the delayed attack was a deliberate decision on the part of the wolves. This event provokes questions about wolves' forethought, memory, and decision-making processes, and also argues that a wolf's instinct may be outweighed by passion.[16]

The Hunter

Depending upon the circumstances, a wolf will eat almost anything, from mice to bison. Larger wolves rely heavily on large, hoofed animals for their sustenance, whereas smaller wolves (such as the red wolf) and lone wolves will have a more varied diet that includes smaller mammals. Wolves have been known to eat white-tailed deer, moose, elk, musk ox, Dall sheep, Rocky Mountain sheep, mountain goats, mule deer, pronghorn antelope, swamp rabbits, hares, javelina, fiddler crabs, raccoons, prairie dogs, caribou, beaver, bison, flightless ducks, marmots, mice, squirrels, nutria, mink, muskrats, grouse, geese, rabbits, salmon, arctic grayling, whitefish, snakes, lizards, insects, grass (which is believed to clean their intestines of worms), berries, and (rarely) domestic stock.

43

Attached to the lower back of the massive jaw is the masseter muscle, which attaches to the zygomatic arch and provides the force needed to cut and grind flesh or bone while the jaw is almost closed. The temporalis muscle wraps around and is attached to a ridge on the top of the skull behind the eye sockets; it is used when the jaws are open, allowing wolves to apply the pressure necessary to suffocate or hold on to prey. The sharp tips, high cusps, and jagged edges of the carnassial teeth work like powerful shears to cut flesh. The incisors are used to gnaw bones but are also capable of gentle grooming. The molars and premolars are used for chewing and crushing bone.

WOLVES AS SCAVENGERS: Scavenging has proved vital to the wolf's survival, especially considering the low success rate in attempted kills (10 percent, according to one study).[17] With their short, efficient digestive tract, wolves are built to eat both fresh and rotten meat. Their reliance on scavenging varies greatly. One study in Algonquin Park showed that out of thirty moose carcasses eaten by wolves, only four were actually killed by wolves; the rest of the moose had died from starvation, old age, or parasites. Life in the wild is difficult and harsh; prey is hard to find. In a sad display of the changes in wolf behavior due to their proximity to humans, Arctic wolves on Ellesmere Island (near the Eureka weather station) and wolves in Europe have learned to feed at local dumps.

After a successful hunt, a one-hundred-pound wolf can consume twenty pounds of meat at one sitting and then survive for weeks without food. The average wolf needs to eat five pounds of food a day in winter and two and a half pounds in the summer, the equivalent of approximately fifteen deer per year.

Temporary Alpha

Usually wolves are not particularly aggressive around the kill, although this may sound improbable when thirteen hungry wolves are involved. In such a situation, the wolf pack seems to have an instinctive morality. A temporary change in dominance has been observed when one member of the pack has clear possession of food and the others do not, even if that wolf is younger and weaker than the rest. Rather than taking the food away forcefully, the others watch the wolf eat, showing subordination. This practice seems to prevent fights. This rule is enforced by the pack, for when food is stolen the perpetrator is threatened. This does not mean that wolves with food will necessarily gorge all of it themselves: one wolf seen eating a bird in front of his drooling sister rose in the middle of his meal and deposited the uneaten half near her.

A failure rate as high as 90 percent
is recorded in studies of
wolves' hunting attempts.

Finding Prey

Commonly wolves find suitable prey by tracking it, scenting it, or simply by coming across it. There are also recorded cases where wolves seemed to know where the prey was and hunted with a definite direction in mind. Wolves have been known to take shortcuts to intercept caribou that are two days ahead of them—with astonishing accuracy.

Finding prey in expansive wolf territory can be especially complex. In order to overcome this challenge, a large pack will often split up to cover more ground. If one of the hunting groups makes a kill, all of the other pack members find or are led to the kill. By fanning out to cover a larger area and then coming together to attack prey once it is found, wolves are able to cover much more territory.

Only experience teaches a wolf how to hunt as part of a group. To successfully hunt with the pack, wolves must learn to observe and cooperate, and must know when to pursue or give up the chase. Each wolf must be conscious of where its pack members are during the hunt, continually reading their movements. It would be impossible for wolves to take down large prey without working together.

While hunting, wolves can be gored, kicked, or trampled, resulting in cracked skulls, fractured ribs, broken bones, internal bleeding, or death. Up to 90 percent of hunting attempts fail. Because of the dangers involved in the hunt, young wolves learn that the sick, old, young, or injured are easiest to catch, and they will look for these animals first.

Testing Prey

A wolf will stalk its intended prey in order to get as close as possible. When the animal detects the wolf's presence it will run away, stand its ground, or, rarely, approach the predator. Moose, elk, and musk oxen are likely to stand their ground if not somehow weakened, whereas deer and smaller prey must run since they are not strong enough to defend themselves. Biologists

believe that the sight of an escaping animal is a stimulus for the wolf to pursue; if the prey stands its ground, wolves commonly abandon the hunt.

Wolves will test a herd by chasing them; this helps the wolves find the animals that are weakest. Canids process vision more quickly than humans—for instance, they would see the rapidly flickering frames

broadcast through a television as individual images—
which enables them to notice an individual with a
slight limp in a whirl of stampeding animals. This act
of testing the prey spares wolves a lot of effort, energy,
and injury. If wolves are unable to detect an animal
that the pack is likely to catch, they will abandon the
hunt and move on. The chase is commonly very
short; wolves will often give up after an unsuccessful
half-mile pursuit. Typically, one or two wolves chase

the animal from behind while others flank the prey
on each side. If the prey pauses at an obstacle or turns,
the flankers are there to intercept and they will attack,
concentrating on the rump, flanks, shoulder, nose,
and neck. Though the wolf has been accused of being
unnecessarily violent with its prey, when a wolf attacks
one animal the others of the herd often stand by and
watch, apparently unaffected. Death is a part of daily
life for all animals living in the wild.

Wolves and other Animals

Civilized man often fails to realize that he is merely a link in the chain of life. The wolf is also part of the natural order and is vital to its balance. Every year approximately $20 million in taxpayers' money is spent in the United States in an effort to control the population of coyotes, which are naturally kept in check when wolves are present. In four years, Yellowstone Park wolves reduced the coyote population by 30 percent. Wolves can also aid coyotes and other predators (brown bear, black bear, foxes, wolverines, ravens, and other carnivores) by providing kills to scavenge. It has been observed that when a wolf is near a herd, the weakened animals are the first to show signs of stress. In some cases animals are so old and decrepit that wolves are simply overeager scavengers, killing animals that are near death.

Eliminating wolves affects both prey and fellow predators. Predators maintain herd quality by killing the sick, the inferior, and the additional young produced by all prey species in anticipation of predation. The predator prevents overgrazing and overpopulation, which can lead to mass starvation.

By keeping prey populations normal and by feeding scavengers, the wolf plays a vital and complex role as the main nonhuman predator of large animals in the Northern Hemisphere. Without the wolf, the balance of the ecosystem is thrown askew.

Raven and Wolf

Wolves and ravens have a unique relationship. Wolves follow ravens in hope of finding carrion, and ravens in turn lead wolves to live prey. Ravens are believed to rely on wolves and other scavengers to break the tough skin of carcasses. The call of the raven serves as a dinner bell to wolves and vice versa. One researcher even discovered that birds came when he imitated a howl.[18] The raven jumps in after the wolves finish with a kill or sometimes the two eat together, wolf on one end, raven on the other. Ravens eat large amounts of meat. If a wolf does not cache its meat it will most likely return to find the carcass picked clean by ravens.

One hunter saw three wolves traveling together, a raven flying above their heads. One wolf suddenly swerved, his body stiffening. His legs seemed paralyzed and gave out from beneath him. The wolf lay stark and stiff on the ground. The other wolves moved on and the raven landed near the wolf, hopping over to peck at the animal. Before the raven had a chance to peck at the wolf again, the animal snapped to life and closed its jaws on the bird![19] The following ex-cerpts depict similar "playful" interactions between these two highly intelligent animals.

"Shawano [a captive wolf] became interested in a raven that flew down and landed on one of the enclosure's fence posts. . . . Bird and wolf stared at one another for some moments. Then Shawano heard something in another direction and, distracted, turned to look. Immediately upon the wolf's eyes leaving the raven, the large black bird flew down and actually landed on Shawano's back, causing the almost fully grown, future leader of the pack to jump as though he had received an electric shock. The raven merely touched down on the wolf's back and immediately flew upward again, but the experience quite unnerved Shawano, who had yet to realize that these big, tough northern birds have enjoyed a special relationship with wolves since time immemorial."[20]

—R. D. Lawrence, In Praise of Wolves

"The birds would dive at the wolf's head or tail, and the wolf would duck and then leap at them. Sometimes the ravens chased the wolves, flying just above their heads, and once, a raven waddled to a resting wolf, pecked at its tail, and jumped aside as the wolf snapped at it. When the wolf retaliated by stalking the raven, the bird allowed it within a foot before arising. Then it landed a few feet beyond the wolf and repeated the prank."[21]

—David Mech, The Wolf

"[The raven] let the pups trot to within six feet of him, then rose and settled a few feet away to await them again. He played this raven tag for ten minutes at a time. If the wolves ever tired of it, he sat squawking till they came over to him again."[22]

—Lois Crisler, Arctic Wild

Wolves of Myth

Our understanding of wolves is continually evolving.
What was once believed to be the ultimate truth about wolves
is what we now call mythology. Throughout history, our
understanding of the wolf has woven in and out of ignorance.
We have moved from an innate knowledge of the wolf's behavior
—from a perspective so close we believed the animal was our kin—
to understanding so little about the wolf that we believe it to
be evil, malicious, and full of hatred for humans.

A myth often tells us more about the culture that created it than about its subject. Myths of the wolf were commonly manufactured to serve specific ends. From its inception, the Christian church, for example, has portrayed the wolf in its scriptures and teachings as a symbol of evil in order to teach morals. Scientific texts of the Middle Ages, whose content was controlled by the church, set forth that the wolf had not seven but only one cervical vertebra: that its backbone was entirely stiff. This characteristic was thought to be a physical manifestation of the wolf's inflexible nature. Firsthand observation would have quickly disproved this "scientific data," yet even reputable scientists Aristotle and Pliny subscribed to this belief.[1] Perhaps the power of the symbol was so strong that scientists did not trouble themselves with sorting fact from fiction.

When similar myths arise in unrelated cultures, it is likely that they originated in observation of wolf behavior. For example, in Europe, America, and Japan, the wolf has been regarded as a fertility god for crops, a belief that may have originated in the wolf's predation of mice and other animals that are regarded as pests. The presence of wolves thus allowed the crops to grow and mature for harvest.

"... this wild brotherhood, pastoral and rural, of priests dressed as wolves began before civilization and laws."
—Marcus Tullius Cicero, Roman statesman, describing the Lupercalia festival in the speech *Pro Caelio*, 56 B.C.

Fertility

Though a predator, the wolf has been associated with fertility in many cultures. For example, at shrines dedicated to the wolf, the Japanese Shinto offered the animal gifts and sacrifices in return for fertile crops. This tradition continues today in the form of prayer plaques with the image of the wolf god, *Okuchi-no-kami* ("the deity with the open mouth").[3]

🌾 The Grain Wolf: German, French, and Slavic nations believed that the last sheaf left on the field was inhabited by the field spirit, a wolf that held a fertilizing power in its tail. Whoever cut or bound that sheaf was said to take on the fertility power and to adopt the fearsome aspects of the wolf. Possessed by the wolf spirit, this person would run amok in the village, frightening children and biting people, and could only be placated by meat. The last sheaf would be shaped into a figure and used as the centerpiece of the harvest celebration. It was either preserved through the winter or destroyed to ensure fertility in the following growing season. The act of destroying the figure is believed to be a remnant of human and animal sacrifices

meant to ensure future fertility. It has been suggested that one purpose of belief in the wolf spirit was to frighten children away from the fields so that they would not trample the crops.

🌾 The Green Wolf, Grass Wolf, or Pea Wolf: In France, an annual summer fire festival was traditionally held for this fertility king and his brotherhood.

🌾 In Ancient Rome and Greece, the Lupercai (the unification of the priestly colleges of *luper* ["wolf"] and *cus* ["goat"]) were said to serve the god Faunus, the protector of domestic flocks from wolves. The celebration of Lupercalia is believed to be the origin of Valentine's Day: on February 15, bands of young men assigned to either the goat or wolf fraternity ran through crowds of spectators creating havoc and whipping young women with leather thongs made from the skin of sacrificed goats. The whipping was thought to make the town's women fertile.

Wolf represented in a carved Pictish stone from Scotland-Ardross, seventh century. Inverness Museum.

In a Roman marriage custom, the newlywed wife anointed her husband's bedpost with wolf fat in hopes of increased fertility.

Painted ware from Triopolye dated 5000 to 3500 B.C. depicts wolves flying over and protecting seeds or heavenly plantings.

The wolf was sacred to Mars when he served as the Greco-Roman god of agriculture, spring, fertility, and growth in nature, and as protector of cattle. Some sources cite Mars as the father of Romulus and Remus, the legendary founders of Rome who were cared for by a she-wolf.

What is not commonly known about this sculpture, which has been the totem of the city of Rome for centuries, is that the children (Romulus and Remus) were added to the sculpture in 1400, although the wolf was sculpted at some time between 500 and 480 B.C. This sculpture is one of the earliest European examples of large, hollow, bronze statuary. Though it has never been questioned that this animal represents a wolf, there are many features that are quite unlike a wolf's. The mane is sculpted like a lion's mane and the lack of fur on the body is reminiscent of a dog. The sensitive expression of the eyes depicts a human expression of fear. Though some have interpreted the wolf's slack jaw as a snarl, when compared to an actual wolf's expressions it appears that the animal's mouth is open with nervous panting. Museo Capitolino, Rome.

"Nine kings to Odin's wide domain were sent, by Hakon's right hand slain! So well the raven-flocks were fed—So well the wolves were filled with dead!"

—Thorleif Raudfeldson, thirteenth-century Scandinavian poet[5]

In this Viking picture stone from the Isle of Man, Fenris fulfills the apocalyptic prophecies by eating Odin.

The Wolf and the Viking

In ancient Scandinavia, warriors called *ulvhethnar* (wolf shirts) were known for being fearless to the point of insanity. They did not wear chain mail in battle, instead donning animal skins, an early form of armor. Those who wore the wolf's skin were believed to adopt the formidable attributes of that animal: they would howl like wolves, gain superhuman strength, and bite their own shields in wild excitement. These warriors also attempted to gain the strength of a wolf by drinking its blood: "Straight away bring your throat to its steaming blood and devour the feast of its body with ravenous jaws. Then new force will enter your frame, an unlooked-for vigor will come to your muscles, an accumulation of solid strength soak through every sinew."[4]

These wolf warriors are thought to have worked closely as a determined pack, using skill in deception. In contrast, bear warriors (called *berserkers*, from which comes our word *berserk*) were loners able to summon up a blind rage, striking down all that stood in their way. These animal totems are thought to have represented the raiding party (wolves) and the outstanding champion (bear). The intensity and ferocity with which the Vikings fought shocked Romans and Byzantines, who had by then adopted more "civilized" battle tactics.

The wolf often appears in Teutonic myth as a fearsome beast that plays an important role in death and in the apocalypse. The following myth of Fenris the wolf reflects the idea that order can only be established when the chaotic and destructive potential of the earth is fettered. In other words, man can only be civilized when the wilderness is controlled, or when the wild part of his own personality is kept in check.

Fenris the wolf, born of the evil god Loki, lived in the heavens with the gods. At his birth, prophets warned that this creature would devour the chief god, Odin, but the gods thought him no different than other wolves. It was decided that the bravest god, Tyr, would look after and feed him.

Fenris grew larger by the day, and it soon became apparent that he was no ordinary wolf. The gods began to fear the powerful wolf, but could not kill him because his evil blood would stain the heavens. Instead, they devised a plan to chain him. Out of iron they forged the strongest chain ever, known as Laeding. Showing this to Fenris, they asked him if he believed that he was as strong as Laeding. "Surely it is strong, but I am stronger," Fenris said, and agreed to be chained as a test of strength. The gods set about chaining the enormous wolf, and when they were done, Fenris tightened the muscles in his great body and snapped the chains that bound him.

Determined to find a way to trap the great wolf, the gods had another chain forged that was double the strength of Laeding and thicker than one of Fenris's massive legs. This chain was known as Droma. Fenris craved to be recognized and feared so he accepted this new challenge. The wolf's effort was torturous; he writhed, twisted, flexed, and suffered in his struggle against the chains. Fenris seemed sure to be trapped.

Then, with one great crack, the chain broke into splinters. Surely now they could not find a stronger chain to save Odin from his fate in the jaws of the enormous wolf.

For the next chain the gods traveled deep under the earth to where the trolls lived. Asked to make the strongest fetter in the world, the trolls made Gleipner, constructed of women's beards, the roots of mountains, the sound of a cat's footfall, the sinews of a bear, the breath of fish, and the spit of birds. This silken thread was presented to the gods, and they brought this new fetter to the wolf. Fenris was as unsure of the deceptively simple rope as the gods were; however, for fear of being called a coward he complied with their request. His sole condition to being bound was that

one of the gods must put his wrist in the wolf's mouth as a guarantee that he would be released. Tyr boldly placed his hand in the wolf's cavernous mouth.

Though Fenris flexed and fought, the binding that held him only grew stronger with his struggle. In one great strain against the silken thread he snapped Tyr's wrist off at the joint. The great wolf was trapped.

The myth tells that Fenris will remain bound until the end of time, when the two wolves that chase the sun and the moon through the sky will catch and devour the glowing ball and the silver sphere, and chaos will ensue. Only then will the ribbon that binds the great wolf Fenris burst, and to fulfill the prophecy, Fenris will devour Odin, bringing the known world to an end.

Wolf devouring man. Detail of a pine pew from Torpo Church, 1200. Hallingdal Buskerud, Norway.

Petroglyph of men with wolves' ears
and tails playing lutes. Found in cave
on island of Gotland, Sweden.

Wolf Clans

As early as the Upper Paleolithic period, humans have yearned for the power of animals, and have gone to great lengths to *become* the wolf: not to imitate the animal but rather to appropriate its instincts and traits. Only upon embracing the entire being's essence could a human gain the wolf's insight or magic. It is known that while hunting, Native Americans would wear wolf skins in order to move about unnoticed in herds of prey. To absorb the spirit of the wolf, humans have donned wolf skins (belts, hats, cloaks), drunk wolf blood, eaten wolf parts, anointed themselves with magical ointments, and even worn wolves' heads atop their own heads. If any strength was gained from these rituals it was surely summoned from the potency of belief.

The following summaries of legends and beliefs illustrate the age-old longing for the magic of the wolf:

- Cro-Magnon paintings, which depict man-beast transformations, often include a wolf tail or head that was probably intended to enable the wearer to summon the knowledge or strength of wolves. Several paintings of a man with a wolf's head and a wolf's tail appear around Lake Onega in Siberia. In one painting this shaman carries a disk and a crescent, believed to represent the sun and the moon. Such depictions of wolf shamans continued throughout early pastoral and agricultural societies.
- In the fifth century B.C., Greek dramatist Euripides described Dolan, a Trojan spy disguising himself to walk unknown among his enemies: "On my back I will attach a wolf skin, on my head I will put the open jaws of the beast, to my hands I will apply the front paws, and to my legs the rear paws. . . ."[6] However, Dolan did not succeed with his disguise and was decapitated. Scholars believe this event hearkens back to early mask rituals in which initiates suffered a symbolic death in order to gain admittance into a wolf clan.
- In Turkish myth, Tura, the nation's founder, was born of a she-wolf. The wolf was a national totem on banners and flags before conversion to Islam. The Turks even called themselves "Sons of the Wolf."
- Wolf-warrior clans have existed in many regions, including Iran, Scandinavia, Mongolia, Rome, India, and America.
- Early Indo-European warrior societies had wolf deities, and are known to have identified with wolves.
- The Sicilians thought that wolves' heads, when worn, gave the wearer courage, while Girgentis of the southern coast of Sicily believed that children who wore shoes made of wolf skin would grow up to become strong and brave.
- Members of the Tonkawa tribe of the Southern Plains believed that they came into being with the help of a wolf that released their ancestors from under the earth by scratching away the soil. The wolf was celebrated and emulated by this tribe.

Rho-shaped plaque of a tiger fighting a mythical wolf, 300 B.C. From the Siberian gold treasure of Peter the Great, Hermitage, Leningrad.

Wolf-coats they are called,

those who carry blood-

stained swords to battle;

they redden spears when

they come to the slaughter,

acting together as one."

—Hrafnsmál, 900 A.D.

- Cormac Airt, mythical king of Ireland, was said to have been suckled and accompanied by wolves. He was also known as Ulfhota (*Ulf* means "wolf").
- In Greek mythology, Lycastus and Parrhasius (the sons of Ares) were thrown into a river by their mother, who feared the children's father. The river god brought the babies into the hollow of an oak tree, where they were suckled by a she-wolf until a shepherd found them and carried them home.
- In the Persian religion of Zoroastrianism, the Mairya were a clan associated with sorcery and known as carrion eaters. The Zoroastrian scriptures called them "two-footed wolves, worse than the four-footed kind."[7]
- The Volsunga saga, a prose story written in Iceland in the twelfth or thirteenth century, speaks of young heroes who lived in the forest. They were said to support themselves like wolves, i.e., through robbery and killing.
- The Greek historian Herodotus reported that the Neuri, a western Russian nomadic tribe, were believed to be sorcerers who changed into wolves for a few days each year.
- Morocco had its own werewolf clans that ate carrion and vermin as wolves do.
- The Lukoi, a wolf cult of Acadia, were said to have practiced the rites of Zeus Lycaeus: devotees ate a wolf in order to absorb the animal's essence.
- Upper Paleolithic hunting societies identified with wolves, used them as their totem figures, and considered themselves descendants of the animals.
- The Männerbund, a band of warriors in the Baltic, were followers of a wolf god. After a ritual ingestion of sacred intoxicants, members of the Männerbund waged war and committed murder in a near-hallucinatory state, believing that they and their fellow clansmen were ravening wolves.
- Shamans of the Saami, nomadic people of northern Scandinavia and northwestern Russia, were rumored to habitually turn themselves into wolves, a task considered easier to accomplish prior to the murder of innocent people.
- In ancient Greece the Maenads (women of the orgiastic cult of Dionysus) raised the "beast within" in their ecstasies, and wore wolf masks for their hunts in the forest.

Detail of bronze plaque representing a man clad in wolfskin armor, seventh century.
Staten's Historiska Museum, Stockholm.

Masters of the Wolf

In many cultures, gods who served as the protectors of creatures both wild and domestic were associated with the wolf. This connection may have arisen from the fact that the wolf is an integral link in the food chain: the wolf controls and is controlled in turn by the population of the species it preys upon. Looking at how wolves chase and test their prey, the wolf can easily be interpreted as the animals' master. This is how wolves were perceived early on in the Great Plains of America; Meriwether Lewis of the Lewis and Clark expedition called the wolf the "shepherd of the buffalo."

◈ In Russian folklore, Leshii was the guardian of the forest and the beasts that resided there. Leshii's favorite animal was the wolf, and on occasion, he would himself take the form of a large white wolf. This deity was even said to shepherd entire flocks of wolves.

◈ Lascoweic, a Slavic wolf spirit that protected the wild animals, was known as the "master of the wolves." He was portrayed either as a wolf or as a stag riding a wolf.

◈ The Russian Saami people treated the wolf very roughly in order to scare the spirit who guarded the animals into keeping them under control.

◈ Faunus, the Italic half-man-half-goat deity of the fields and herds, was called a wolf god, but was also said to ward off wolves, protecting both livestock and wildlife.

◈ Mars, the god of crops and fertility (later known as the god of war), was in charge of the borders between farms and wild lands, and was said to defend the crops and herds from attacks by untamed nature. The Italians connected Mars with the wolf: the god was said to have been accompanied by two wolves, Fuga and Timor (the personifications of flight and fear).

◈ St. Nicholas and St. George were both said to be the wolf's patron saints. The forest was avoided on St. George's feast day (November 26), as wolves were thought to be especially active and dangerous. St. George gave the wolf permission to eat, and a common Russian saying was: "If the wolf has something between his teeth, George gave it." Thus, it was believed that a shepherd who lost an animal to the wolf had somehow displeased the saint.

◈ On the eve of St. Andrew's feast, European villagers went into the woods howling through clay pots to attract wolves, feeding them meat in the hope that it would appease the animals.

◈ Artemis (sometimes addressed as Artemis *Lycea*, or "wolfish"), a "lady of beasts," is the Grecian goddess of the hunt, the moon, night, and nature. A wolf was emblazoned on her shield.

Inner plates of the Gundestrup Cauldron depicting Cerennunos (protector of animals both domestic and wild) flanked by a wolf, c. 100 B.C. Silver-plated copper. National Museet, Copenhagen.

"A wolf caught a sheep, and when the shepherd chased it, the wolf said, 'Who will be its guard on the day of wild beasts, when there will be no shepherd for it except me?'"

—Bukhari,
(Islamic scholar)
Sahih, c. 850

Painted wood Inuit mask of a wolf head. Collected from St. Michael, Alaska. Phoebe A. Hearst Museum of Anthropology, University of California at Berkeley.

The Ainu

Well known for their worship of the bear, the Ainu, native people of Japan, also had a strong respect for the wolf. The wolf is difficult to hunt with traps and spring bows, said the Ainu, since "the animals appear to understand these things nearly as well as the people who set them."[8] The Ainu also found hunting wolves difficult because the animals were shy and fleet of foot.

According to the Ainu, wolves would only attack humans with great provocation, and would even help humans in distress. Dreaming of a wolf, or simply of its howl, was said to have such strength that it could cure any illness. If pursued by an "evil bear," a human should loudly call upon the wolf for help. If performed with a true heart, this plea for help would be quickly answered. the wolf would kill the bear, freeing the man.

The Ainu saw the divine wolf of myth as a great being that merited worship. The wolf deity was considered precious, quick in action, and brave. Having abandoned his home in Paradise because of a great desire to live on earth, the divine wolf, clothed in white, was believed to live with the good bears on the east side of the mountains.

The Sacred Wolf

Native Americans' connection to the wolf is very similar to that of other primitive peoples; they had great respect for the animal. One band of the Kwakiutl believed that its ancestors were wolves who survived a giant flood by escaping to a mountaintop. There they shed their skins and became men and women.

- Many Native American tribes believed that the wolf's power could be transferred to humans. They made sacred wolf bundles, healed themselves with wolf power, named themselves or their clans after the wolf, and adopted the wolf spirit as their guardian. According to the Inuit belief, the power of the wolf resides everywhere (in the sky, water, and land), not just in the animal itself. To most Native American tribes, the wolf served as a medium between humans and the Great Unknown.

- The Yupiaq respected the wolf for its social organization, and the people of Vancouver Island believed that the wolf had a supernatural community of its own that employed the raven as storyteller. Native Americans were well aware that in the wild, the wolf held a strong position in relation to other animals, providing food for scavengers. The wolf's howl was believed to call other animals to the kill intentionally: foxes, ravens, coyotes, and even humans, who would chase the wolves away and steal a fresh kill.

- The Native American people understood that wolves were an important part of the ecosystem. Wolves were believed to be as complex as humans, with their own individual strengths and weaknesses, with both good and evil in their nature.

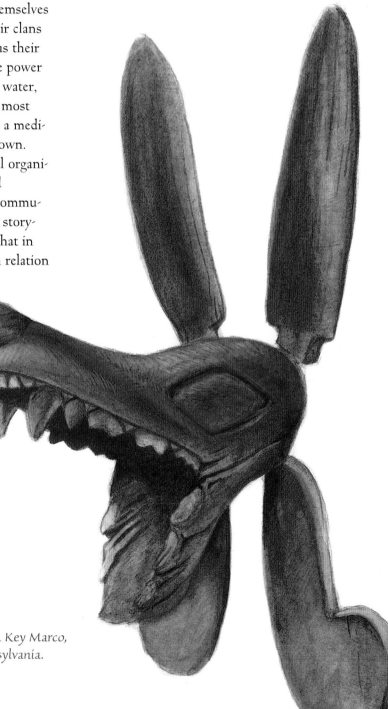

Pre-Columbian wooden mask of a red wolf from Key Marco, Florida. University Museum, University of Pennsylvania.

Kwakiutl wolf dancer wearing a mask of wood and bone.

Who Will Speak for the Wolf?

A traditional oral poem tells of a time that the Oneida tribe had to relocate because the land was becoming overcrowded. The tribe quickly chose a new place to live without taking into account its large population of wolves. After a short time, the wolves became increasingly bold, approaching the edge of the village more and more frequently, and the men had to spend much of their time chasing them away. They knew that with a great deal of effort over a number of years, they could kill the wolves, and almost decided to follow that route. After much consideration, they decided that they did not desire to become people who adapted the land to suit themselves, but preferred to be a part of the world's natural order. They moved, leaving the land to the wolves. Whenever the Oneida Nation again pondered whether an action was necessary or excessive, someone would rise and ask, "Tell me now my brothers! Tell me now my sisters! Who speaks for the Wolf?"

Detail of a Greek amphora depicting Leto giving birth to Apollo, flanked by two wolves.

Lukos and Luke

The Greek words for "wolf" (*lukos*) and "light" (*luke*) are very similar, and have been intertwined in mythology. The ancient peoples who lived in the countries bordering the Baltic and Norwegian Seas believed that the wolf was an animal of light. It is to the wolf that these people dedicated the constellation we know as Ursa Major, the Great Bear. Scholars believe that the Greeks developed their myth of Phoebus Apollo from the myths of the north, which connect the wolf with light.

In Apollo's legendary autumnal journeys to the far north, he encountered the creatures dedicated to him: the wolf and the swan. Legend told that a wolf came to Apollo's mother, Leto (who personified night), when she was pregnant, and thus the essence of the solar wolf was passed into Apollo. In the same way that the sun is born of the night, Apollo was born of Leto. As a result of that encounter, Apollo's surname became Lukogenes, meaning "born of the wolf." Apollo appeared on occasion in the form of the wolf, which was considered one of his sacred beasts. At Lycopolis, the fifth-century Roman philosopher and mythographer Macrobius wrote that "the wolf was revered as a representation of Apollo." To further strengthen this connection (which has often been debated), Macrobius wrote "The Wolf who is the Sun" when speaking of ancient peoples who employed the wolf as a representation of the sun.

Lycaon

The myth of Lycaon is one of the earliest recorded accounts of werewolf transformation. It is from Lycaon that we get the word *lycanthropy* (assumption of the form of a wolf by witchcraft or by magic) and the subspecies name for the Eastern Timber Wolf (*Canis lupus lycaon*).

According to this myth, upon hearing of men who were disrespectful of both the mortal and the divine, Zeus, father of the gods in Greek mythology, visited the earth in disguise. He came upon a banquet hall in which King Lycaon and his nobles were eating and drinking.

The king noticed the dejected-looking peasant standing at the door and said, "If you have come to beg for food, I will allow you to do tricks for my servants. Go and await your scraps outside the gates." To this Zeus approached the feast table and replied, almost unable to contain his anger, "The God of all the heavens holds the traveler and the beggar dear. It is appropriate for you to show some respect, for I stand before you as Zeus!"

King Lycaon, scoffing at the stranger, answered, "Then join us in our feast, Zeus!" He stood, grabbed the freshest plate of meats, brought it to Zeus, and set it before the god with great flourish.

Zeus recoiled in disgust at the sight of the human organs and limbs set before him by the king. Flames flew up from around Zeus as his presence suddenly filled the massive hall. All around Lycaon lay his companions, struck dead by the god's mighty power. Lycaon's body contorted in pain, and he was thrown to the floor,

but he could not take his eyes off the god who continued to grow before him.

When Zeus turned to leave, Lycaon became aware of a raw hunger twisting inside him. He yearned for warm flesh and blood. He tried to rise but remained crouched on the floor: in place of his hands were huge, hairy paws, and he had grown a long, bushy tail. In fear, he screamed a howl more horrid than the earth had ever known.

King Lycaon quickly grew accustomed to his new shape. After all, he had always had the black heart of the wolf.

Late-sixteenth-century engraving depicting Lycaon transformed to the "living picture of ferocity" by Zeus.

Mirrored detail of Celtic wolves from Ardagh Chalice, Limerick. Ireland, eighth century.

Coursing Through the Skies

Another folkloric role of the wolf was to announce night, winter, and the apocalypse. This representation of change and destruction could have originated in the wolf's habit of being active at dusk, a time when humankind would lose the life-giving sun and would grow increasingly uncomfortable with the coming darkness.

- In the *Edda*, a collection of Old Norse poems assembled in the thirteenth century, twilight is called the shadow or the ear of the wolf.
- German mythology mentions gods who enter into wolves' skins, representing the sun hiding itself either in the night or in the snowy season of winter (as in the Apollo myth, where the solar hero becomes the wolf).
- The wolf is depicted on a Breton-issue coin ingesting or spitting out the sun and the moon, which has been interpreted as the death and rebirth of the world. Similarly, northern Gaulish coins portray the wolf devouring the sun, which is thought to symbolize the priest's or ruler's control of the supernatural.
- In Celtic myth, the trickster god Lok took the shape of a wolf as a great destroying power of the universe.
- The Kirgis, people of the Central Asian Steppes, called Ursa Major's seven stars "watchmen," and believed that they guarded two "horses" (large stars) held by ropes (the Little Bear and the pole star) and stalked by a wolf. The end of the world would come when the wolf finally succeeded in killing the horses.
- The Blackfoot and Pawnee Native American tribes called the Milky Way the "Wolf Road," and believed it to be a path worn across the heavens by the spirits of their dead ancestors.
- In a Norse myth, the wolf Hati ("hate") chased Mani (the moon), who drove his chariot through the sky. Hati closed in on Mani every month, causing the waxing and the waning of the moon. In a companion myth, the wolf Skoll was said to chase Sol (the sun, Mani's brother) through the sky. During solar or lunar eclipses, it was thought that the wolf had caught up to the chariot, and either the sun or moon was in danger of being eaten. To save the endangered celestial orb, humans would frighten the wolf away by pounding pots and pans.
- The Yakut of eastern Siberia, in the Lena River region, believed that bears and wolves caused the waning of the moon by gnawing on its disc.
- Darkness-loving Slavic werewolves called *vîrcolac* were said to eat the sun and the moon, causing eclipses.
- In Teutonic myth, the gigantic wolf Managram will drink the blood of the dead, swallow the moon, and cover the sky with blood to announce the end of the world.

This painting from a cave near Lake Onega, Russia, is thought to depict a sorcerer with a wolf's head and tail. Since a similar figure appears several times in this region this image is believed to represent a myth; the disk and crescent may symbolize the sun and moon.

- The mythological wolf of the Celts was also believed to bring on the night by swallowing the sun.
- Dusk—neither daylight nor darkness—has been called the time between the dog and the wolf both in Latin *(Inter canem et lupum)* and French *(Entre chein et loup)*. The wolf symbolized night, the unknown, and wilderness. A similar folk saying was used in Sweden for the hours before dawn, which were called "the hours of the wolf."
- In pre-Christian times, people of Baltic countries held that wolves gained supernatural strength and ferocity from electrical storms, shooting stars, comets, and the moon. From such celestial sources, the wolf was also given strange insight and otherworldly forces. The wolf was also said to have sniffed amber in order to gain power and communication with celestial forces. In the seventeenth century it was declared scientific fact that the size of the wolf's brain increased and decreased with the waxing and waning of the moon.[9]
- According to prophesies of the ancient *Avesta*, the sacred text of Zoroastrianism, upon the apocalypse (estimated to be circa 2000 A.D.) the earth will cry out, "I cannot endure this demon, which is indeed hidden, I cannot endure its habitation in me, for it seizes me with such scarification, and tears me like the four-legged wolf when it tears the belly of beneficent animals from them, and seizes their young." And upon the end of the known world all wolf species of the earth will go to one place, and will become one. The Mazda-Zoroaster worshippers would have to fight this monster wolf, which would be the breadth of 415 paces and the length of 433 paces.[10]

This Etruscan tomb painting depicts Hades wearing a wolf skin.

Wolves and Death

It is likely that humans have always associated wolves with death. Due to their tendency to eat carrion, wolves have been a prominent fixture in graveyards, battlefields, and in times of plague were even known to have confronted the dead or dying in their homes.

◈ Wolves found eating the remains of the unearthed dead were believed to be attacking vampires (partially decomposed, swollen, and with blood at the mouth, corpses fit the believed description of vampires). Romanian gypsies believed that a white wolf wandered the cemeteries to keep vampires in their graves.

- In biblical depictions of the Day of Judgement the jaws of hell were often depicted as the jaws of a wolf.
- Apollo, said to have been born from the wolf spirit, was once the god of the dead.
- Hecate, the Greek goddess, was depicted with one or three wolf heads; the wolf head symbolized dominion over the underworld. Hecate ruled over the spirits of the dead and of humans who had been returned to Earth. The howling of wolves and trembling of the ground was supposed to herald her arrival.
- Many cultures have viewed the wolf as a guard to the land of the dead. Among them are the Egyptians, Naskapi Cree, and Canadian Inuit.
- The Valkyries, Teutonic maidens of the battlefield, would arrive mounted upon huge wolves to carry away the dead. The wolves then would transport the dead to Vallhalla (the Hall of the Slain) where a wolf stood guard at the western door. A Viking often boasted of his achievements in battle by claiming that he had fed many wolves by leaving slain enemies on the battlefield.
- The wolf is a symbol of evil in the Zoroastrian doctrines from the seventh-century-B.C. Persia, which accentuated the universal struggle between the forces of light and darkness. The animal is said to be a legionary of Ahriman, the spirit of evil, deceit, and wickedness, and is called "the flatterer" or "the deadly wolf."
- The wolf was considered the sacred animal of Mars, the planet of evil, plague, war, and death.
- Upuaut, the wolf god of ancient Egypt, guided the souls of the dead through the dark realm to the underworld.
- In Native American Menominee tribal legend, Moqwaio the wolf (brother of the sun deity Mannabush) was placed in charge of the dead when he was pulled under the sea and drowned by his foe Anamaqkin.
- The Cheyenne believed that by scattering the dead, wolves assisted in carrying the remains of the dead to the Sacred Persons who resided at the four cardinal positions.

- Charon, the ferryman on the river Styx, is depicted with wolf ears in an Etruscan painting. Odin has also appeared wolf-eared as the Teutonic god of death in Volsunga saga.
- In Normandy, horrible spirits were said to haunt cemeteries and to devour corpses in the guise of wolves.
- In Native American belief, the wolf introduces death upon the earth with a tornado he has stolen.
- Finno-Ugrians (people of eastern Europe and western Siberia) believed that the dead haunted the living in the shape of the wolf.
- Rutu, the Saami spirit of plague and torturer of the dead, had a wolf as his hound.
- In a sweat-bath ritual of the Omaha tribe of north-eastern Nebraska, the wolf represents man's restlessness, questioning of fate, and destructiveness.

Hecate with three heads representing dominion over air, earth, and the underworld. The symbol of the wolf's head is employed in later depictions of gods and goddesses of death.

Witch riding a wolf. Wood engraving illustrating Ulrich Molitor's About Witches and Fortune Tellers, *Cologne, France, 1489.*

Witches and Devils

Many cultures connect wolves with the activities of witches and devils. In most cases this negative association arose from mythmakers' fears of other cultures: those who had lost the shamanic and totemistic traditions saw those who practiced such rituals as heathens, and saw their gods as devils. Shamans have often taken on the characteristics of the wolf to travel through the supernatural world. Wolves were known by these people to travel far and often, and it was believed that in their travels, wolves gathered knowledge from other worlds.

When those who practiced early nature religions and worshipped the wolf as their war god attacked more civilized cultures, they would howl like wolves, wear wolf skins, and carry shields emblazoned with the wolf's terrifying image. On the battlefield the wolf was seen as the enemy or the legion of the devil, and as a powerful force in the witchcraft of heathens.

- According to German legend, the devil squats between the eyes of the wolf. It is also said that the devil appears as a black wolf.
- A European legend relates that the devil created the wolf from a stump of wood, with a heart of stone and a chest of roots.
- The Latin term *opprobrium lupula* ("little wolf") signifies "witch."
- Upon hearing a wolf howl, European gypsies would warn, "Take care, it may be a witch."
- In Germany witches were said to have ridden wolves, and in Lorraine, a region of northeastern France, the "witch master" would appear at witches' gatherings (called Sabbaths) in the form of a wolf. According to the confessions of witches, whole Sabbaths changed into wolf packs.
- The Navajo tribe believed that men disguised themselves as wolves to practice witchcraft.
- Old women called *vargamor* who lived in the forests of Sweden were claimed to have powers of sorcery and control over wolves.

- The Russian witch Baba Jaga was said to ride a wolf.
- In biblical texts the devil is said to be the "wolf of hell."
- An old Latvian tale tells of a ten-day march at Christmastide, where Satan in the form of a wolf led thousands of demonic werewolves.

Stone corbel representing the devil with wolf ears in Southwell Cathedral, England, c. 1200.

"The Devil has the nature of a wolf; he always looks with an evil eye upon mankind and continually circles the sheepfold of the faithful of the Church, to ruin and destroy their souls.... The wolf's eyes shine in the night like lamps because the works of the Devil seem beautiful and wholesome to blind and foolish men."

—Aberdeen Bestiary, 1542[11]

Time

Wolves are associated with the change from day to night, from summer to winter, and the ultimate change brought about by death. The wolf is further associated with the most immediate and constant reminder of change, the passage of time. In the act of killing prey, the wolf measures out the time allotted to that animal's presence on earth. The finality of time passing is akin to the concept of being devoured, and both acts bring about the end of a certain cycle. In the symbolism of many cultures, when the wolf finishes devouring the past, he will proceed to devour the present, bringing about the end of the world.

⊕ In *A Historie of Foure-Footed Beastes*, Edward Topsell recorded that when wolves swim they "go into the water two by two, every one hanging upon the other's tail, which they take in their mouths." He thus compares them to the days of the year following one another.

⊕ In Hindu belief, the symbol of the wolf is used to explain the passing of time: the wolf of darkness swallows the quail of daytime and springtime. But the Asvins, gods of medicine, revive the quail and it returns in the morning or in the spring.

⊕ The Roman philosopher and mythographer Macrobius describes a statue of the Egyptian sun god Serapis leading a monster with the head of a lion, a dog, and a wolf—possibly an early version of Cerberus, the two-headed dog of Hades. Macrobius interpreted this beast as representing the three aspects of time. The lion is the courage required for the present, the dog is the comfort that allows thoughts of the future, and the wolf consumes the past.

⊕ German myth tells of the wolf as a devourer of seven little goats that represent the days of the week. On the seventh day, the six already-eaten kids are exchanged for stones in the wolf's belly, and the cycle starts again.

⊕ "Cheating the wolf," an old European phrase that meant "to escape death," is also interpreted as an escape from the grasp of time.

⊕ Ancient Greeks called the year "the one who comes, and is measured out by the wolf."

⊕ A Byzantine book of nature calls the year "wolf go," since the seasons of the year were said to follow each other as closely as wolves passing a river.

A bronze depiction of a mythical wolf from Mongolia, second century B.C.

Storm and Wind

The wolf's howl, its most recognizable characteristic, has been noted by many cultures as resembling what we call the howl of the wind.

❄ The fable of the three little pigs—wherein three pigs try to hide from the wolf that pursues them, but he blows down their various shelters—was born of the ancient connection between wolves and wind.

❄ Gases emanating from the ground were called "wolf" by the people of Greece, who believed that such gases came from the supernatural world.

❄ Odin's wolves, Geri and Freki, represent storm and wind.

❄ Fenris, the wolf of Teutonic myth, is said to be a monster of storm and night whose jaws (clouds) touch both heaven and earth.

❄ According to some myths, Apollo's mother, "the dark-robed Leto," arrived in a storm cloud as a she-wolf.

❄ Kaput, the Iranian storm or wind demon, has the form of the wolf.

❄ In Ancient Greece and Argus, the wolf was a symbol of stormy winds in both text and art.

❄ It was once believed that Vila, eastern Slavonic spirits that appeared in the form of a wolf, were capable of calling forth whirlwinds, hailstorms, and rain.

❄ "The wolves are among the grain" was a common German expression for the wind blowing the grain in the fields.

❄ An old European metaphor for a strong destructive wind is "the wolf." When the wind whistles, it is said that the wolf is sharpening its teeth. When the sun shines while rain is falling, it is said to be "the wolves' wedding."

❄ Khanukh is a wolf that controls fog in Tlingit, or Pacific Northwest Native American, belief.

❄ In Snorri Sturlasson's *Skäldskaparmál*, c.1220 (from the *Prose Edda*, a collection of Viking poetry) the expression *hunthr etha vargr vidar*, "the dog or the wolf blows," serves as a metaphor for wind. In Germany, "wolf" serves as the name for mist or wind. Old German pictures portray wind as the head of a wolf from which gusts issue.

❄ A particularly harsh winter in Sweden is called a "wolf's winter."

❄ Dakota tribal legend tells of a man who sought help from the wolf to conquer an enemy. The wolf taught the man a song. When he howled this song, a wind was created to confuse the enemy. When he howled again a fog rolled in and made the warriors invisible.

❄ In the Vedas, the four books of knowledge that constitute the essence of the Hindu religion, werewolves are associated with weather phenomena.

Opener of the Ways

A wooden head of the god Upuaut. Aegyptisches Museum, Berlin.

The Egyptian god Upuaut, most revered in Egypt's first two dynasties (3200–2700 B.C.), was depicted as a wolf or a wolf-headed man. He was god of the dead, pathfinder for the sun's journey through the underworld, and the god of war. *Canis lupaster* (a now-extinct species of wolf) and its habits of eating carrion, lingering around battlegrounds, and appearing at sunset, almost certainly gave rise to the myths associated with Upuaut. This god was also known as Opoïs Wepwawet and Khenti Amenti.

The meaning of the name *Upuaut* is "opener of the ways," which illustrates the god's role of opening the afterlife to the souls of the dead. In funerary proceedings, represented by either a masked priest or a standard (a pole with a banner or figure), he symbolically guided the dead. As leader of the gods, Upuaut was first in the funeral procession, preceding both the pharaoh and the better-known god Osiris. Once placed by the tomb, Upuaut (in the form of two standards) would stand guard and wait for the soul of the dead to awaken. Upon rebirth, the god would guide and protect the dead person's soul through the dark, treacherous realm of the underworld, and on toward the afterlife.

Upuaut guided the sun in a similar way. Egyptians believed that as the sun approached the western horizon, it began a symbolic death, entering the underworld before being reborn and rising again the next morning. The sun was said to travel the watery heavens by day in the Atet barque and the rivers of the underworld by night in the Sektet barque. At night,

Upuaut piloted the barque through these dark, treacherous waters, towing the sun along the edge of the sky when necessary.

As winter came, the sun stayed in the underworld for longer periods. Egyptologist E. A. Wallis Budge claims that the god Upuaut was the personification of the winter solstice.[12] Upuaut was believed responsible for the sun's absence.

Upuaut found his origin in Upper Egypt as a local god of Lycopolis. He was also worshipped in the ancient and sacred burial grounds of Abydos. In Upper Egypt, shrines were dedicated to Upuaut, and his name was given to their children in the hopes that some of the god's power would help guide them through life. Eventually the wolf god served as a tool to unify the lands of Upper and Lower Egypt by playing a role in the merging of their beliefs. This unification is depicted on the Narmer palette, a historically important relief from Egypt that boasts the victories of King Narmer and illustrates his act of unifying Egypt. The third standardbearer in Narmer's procession carries the symbol of the wolf god. In a composite myth, Osiris, the later god of the dead, was credited as Upuaut's father. When combined, these two gods were known as Sekhemtaui, "Power of the Two Lands," representing the marriage of the two halves of Egypt.

Upuaut also served as a war god. In this capacity, "opener of the ways" referred to the "opening" of a battle. In the art of the time, Upuaut was portrayed guiding the warriors of his tribe into enemy territory. Symbolically, he served as the pharaoh's advance guard in war. Upuaut even appears in early Roman sculpture as a wolf headed soldier, fully clad in armor and carrying weapons. Upuaut would be represented with a mace and bow on the first of the four sacred standards, or on a banner preceding the pharaoh in victory processions.

There seems to be much confusion between the wolf god Upuaut and the jackal god Anubis However, the two gods are distinct: Upuaut was depicted with a gray or white head, and was usually standing, while Anubis was depicted with a black head, and lying down.

Greek wolf coin, silver,
hemidrachma denomination,
c. 468–421 B.C. Argolid, Greece.

Wolf Outlaw

It was said that after a highwayman's death, his soul entered the wolf. Outlaws and highwaymen perpetuated the myth by wearing wolf skins over their armor. By the written laws of the Franks and Normans—specifically, the Anglo-Saxon king Canute (1016–35), Edward the Confessor (1042–66), and Henry I in medieval Europe—a man accused of wrongdoing could be morally and lawfully killed if an authority called for a "wolf's head" upon him.

- King Canute's laws referred to an outlaw as a "verevulf," a man transformed into a wolf through antisocial behavior.
- In the Greek tale describing the origin of the Hirpi Sorani (wolf priests), the people of Socrate were offering a sacrifice to Dis Pater (also known as Pluto, the Celtic/Roman god of the dead and the underworld) when a pack of wolves arrived and snatched bits of the victim's flesh directly from the flames. The celebrants pursued the thieves. After a long chase the wolves disappeared into a cave, out of which a pestilent odor emerged. The smell was so rancid that the wolves' pursuers died, and a plague spread throughout the land. An oracle advised the people to appease the gods by living as wolves. The *hirpi* ("wolf") priests began their worship of Soranus (the Sabine god of death), and adopted a life of banditry, thereby ending the plague.
- Wolves were hung beside criminals on the gallows, which perhaps explains the origin of the old Saxon term for gallows, *vargatreo*, which some translate as "wolf tree."

- According to Denmark's medieval laws, those who committed parricide (the killing of a close relative) were to be hung by the heels next to a live wolf. The wolf was chosen because that animal was believed to murder its fellows wantonly. Thieves were punished similarly, hung by a line through the sinews, with a wolf beside them.

- A Roman convicted of killing his mother would have his face covered with a wolf skin.

- *Warg*, a Middle High German word for "wolf," was used to describe a fugitive criminal who was destined to be hanged. This word is believed to be the root of the word *gewürgt* ("to strangle").

- The Saami had such a strong association between wolves and thieves that when Russians who had robbed and killed in Saami territory were eventually driven back into Russia, they were said to have changed into wolves. The Saami believed that was why wolves were so numerous in Russia and so fierce that they ate humans.

- From the Sutherland region of Scotland came the exclamation *Ulb!* or "You brute!" which evolved from the Old Norse *ulfr* ("wolf").

- The wolf appears in many countries, including France and Germany, as a symbol of the stranger. Recently the term *wolf* has been applied to groups of adolescents who are living off, but are also in some way estranged from, society.

- Ovid, the Roman poet who lived from 43 B.C. to A.D. 17, described the wild tribes that he came across in his journeys (Scythians, Getae, Sarmatians, Bessi, Coralli, Iazyges, and Ciziges) as more like wolves than like men. He considered these people barbarians who lived by their strength rather than by their wits.

- *Loup hole*: a spy hole cut out of the wall or door of a roadside shelter so that travelers could watch for "wolves," or rather, werewolves and other outlaws. This expression is the origin of the modern word "loophole."

- The change in Sweden from respect to hatred of wolves has been recorded in the change of the word used for the animal. The Old Norse word for wolf was the Indo-European word *ulv*, meaning "predator." Many children were named Ulv in hopes that they would eventually have the admirable traits of their namesake: courage, skill in hunting, and strength. However, respect for wolves faded in Sweden, as was the trend in Europe, and the name used for wolves was more commonly *varg* ("outlaw") than *ulv*. People began using the word *varg* because they feared that if they called the wolf by his proper name, he would appear (in the sense of the expression "speak of the devil and he will appear"). This shift from *ulv* to *varg* represents a very clear shift in the perception of the animal. Similarly, the words for wolf in Russian (*volk*) and Serbian (*vuk*) both have the etymological root *robber*.

This wooden ornament from a harness represents the head of a deer in the mouth of a wolf. Late fourth century B.C.

"And those who have chosen the portion of injustice, and tyranny, and violence, will pass into wolves, or into hawks and kites; whither else can we suppose them to go?"
—Plato, Phaedo, 360 B.C.[13]

Werewolf

The legend of the werebeast exists all over the world. In areas where wolves do not reside, the creature would appear in the form of a bear, tiger, shark, hyena, or any animal that inspired fear. Werewolves were thought to be men either overpowered by the beast inside them and forced to give in to their basest urges, or cursed by some magic to live as wolves. The word *werewolf* comes from the root *wer*, an Old English noun meaning "man" (also related to the Latin *vir* of the same meaning).

In Europe during the Inquisition, these creatures were flushed out in the name of God as nonbelievers and devils. Christian saints were even said to have punished sinners by turning them into wolves. Some of the convicted werewolves were guilty of heinous murders, but others were tricked or tortured into confessing. In Lyon, France, in the 1570s a hermit named Gilles Garnier was found scavenging a meal from a dead body. He was brought to court, questioned, and intimidated into confessing that he made a pact with the devil and murdered seven children. In 1573 he was burned as a werewolf. The werewolf hunt was an excuse to rid the land of beggars, heathens, the deformed, epileptics, the mentally disabled, and the insane—anyone considered undesirable. Hundreds of people were pronounced werewolves and burned alive.

Every man (few accused werewolves were women) was believed to struggle with the beast within. This fight between good and evil manifested itself in a virtual plague of "werewolves." The concept of a baser, more primitive self was well illustrated by Plato in his writings about dreams: "When the gentler part of the soul slumbers and the control of reason is withdrawn . . . the wild Beast in us . . . becomes rampant." The wolf within us is further associated in folklore and language with incest, murder, and all other forbidden acts. A tailor burned in Paris in 1595 as a werewolf had sexually and physically abused children to their death, then powdered and dressed their bodies. It is more comforting to believe that the atrocities of which man is capable have their origin in a beast rather than to ascribe them to the complex human mind. Those who believed in werewolves denied the source of humankind's primitive nature.

The frantic werewolf trials of Europe eventually died down. After the arrests, trials, and deaths of dozens of accused werewolves in sixteenth-century France, the court finally declared that lycanthropy, the assumption of the form of a wolf by witchcraft or magic, was a delusion of the insane. From that point on, werewolves were considered by everyone except peasants to be heretics rather than supernatural beings. King James I of England also declared in 1600 that "warwoolfes" were victims of delusion. Without a doubt we recognize now that the true fanatics were those who led the crusade against werewolves.

"In the last days the false prophets and corrupters shall be multiplied, and the sheep shall be turned into wolves, and love shall be turned into hate."

-The Teaching of the Lord to the Gentiles by the Twelve Apostles 2nd c. (also known as Didache)

Arreſt memorable de la Cour de parlemét de Dole, du dixhuiĉtiefme iour de Ianuier, 1574 contre Gilles Garnier, Lyonnois, pour auoir en forme de loup-garou deuoré pluſieurs enfans, & commis autres crimes : enrichy d'aucuns poīĉts recueillis de diuers autheurs pour eſclaircir la matiere de telle transformation.

¶ Imprimé à Sens, par Iean Sauine, 1 5 7 4.

The Gilles Garnier scandal. This is the cover page of a sensationalist newspaper printed in Sens, France, by J. Savine, 1574.

Wolf Children

Wherever wolves live, tales are told of wolves that adopt and care for lost children. The traits of such "wolf children" (and adults) may have been one of the origins of werewolf myths, although it is highly unlikely that any such adoptions took place. It is plausible that the idea of wolf adoption arose from the "wolf like" behavior of certain autistic or abused children: they refused to wear clothes, preferred to eat raw meat, favored darkness, howled, bit their caretakers, and walked on all fours.[14] These children were invariably called wolf children before the mental illness associated with such behavior was understood.

In 1920 in Godamuri, India, two girls, Amala and Kamala, were claimed to have been saved from a wolf den in which they lived with two pups and three adult wolves. These children were described as having many wolflike attributes. The stories about these children, and the diaries of the Reverend Singh, their caretaker, have been carefully studied, and the children's behavior has been attributed to mental illness rather than to any association with wolves.[15]

The Wolf and the Lamb

According to the teachings of the Bible, the creatures of the earth were created to live together peacefully in the Garden of Eden. It was man's original sin that spawned the distinction between predators and prey. Christian scripture teaches that the wolf as we know it is an animal whose behavior was born from our original sin.

The Bible depicted animals as soulless creatures that were either a help or a hindrance to the superior, civilized man. Unquestionably, at the time the Bible was written wolves were a serious obstacle to progress as perceived by humans. Wolves, which attacked domestic animals, were essentially attacking the wealth and status of the animals' owners. Indeed, the wolf threatening the lamb (representative of mankind and civilization) was one of the strongest symbols in the Bible. In Matthew 7:15, Jesus warns his prophets, "I send you forth as lambs among wolves. . . ." and "Beware of false prophets which come to you in sheep's clothing, but inwardly they are ravening wolves." The Bible's use of the wolf to represent evil and heresy was amplified by thousands of sermons, speeches, and literary works from generations of teachings.

Though wolves can perceive no difference between a domestic animal and wild prey, man saw the wolf killing his animal as a malicious act. Since the wolf clearly had no intention to repent for his sin, it was up to the farmer to dispense justice by killing the animal.

It may be difficult for us to imagine that people believed that wolves killed out of malice and evil. Unbelievably enough, during the Middle Ages and into the late eighteenth century, animals were put on trial and put to death for killing humans. Animals were jailed and tortured, their moans and wails taken as confessions of guilt. In Burgundy in 1370, three sows killed a boy and the whole herd was brought to

Seal from the monastery of Mesnil-Saint Loup, Aube, France.

court. Though only the three were put to death, the judge severely criticized the rest for not coming to the boy's defense.[16] It was believed that animals committed crimes deliberately and with full knowledge of the sin and the consequences. Since people had no way to understand the thoughts and behaviors of animals, they extrapolated from their own base urges and morals.

Though many earlier religions had taught that nature or wilderness was God, the Bible depicted the wilderness as barren and godless. Sin and imperfection are bound together in the Bible's teachings as strongly as divinity is bound to perfection. Nature needed man's help to attain perfection. This concept was manifested in perfectly structured gardens (such as those of Versailles) which were believed to have God-given beauty. Nature untamed by man was rough, uncivilized, and useless. In this line of thought, the wolf, considered by many to be the embodiment of all things wild, must be the devil himself. A medieval engraving even goes so far as to depict Christ in combat with a wolf.

This is only one chapter in the history of hatred and misunderstanding that began when man first learned to fear the wolf. The scriptures teach that only God can give or take life, which means that though the devil created the wolf, God gave him life. If we had interpreted the Bible differently, perhaps we could have loved the wolf as a creation of God, and ultimately found peace with all of nature. But wolves grew to represent the evil side of humans, a constant reminder of human weakness and human sins. They were seen as a symbol of untamed nature—the primary hindrance of civilization, peace, wealth, and all that was good and gentle. Eventually

"The wolf pretending to be devout held his psalm-book as a devout human would ... and sat under an almond tree and began reprimanding his cubs for not going to church more often and listening to the sermons." Wood engraving from Ravening Wolves by R. Gobin, 1510.

the symbol fell away and, in the minds of many, the wolf itself became the hindrance of humankind. If only the wolf were gone, there would be endless prosperity, and good would prevail over evil. With the death of the wolf would come the death of the beast in man. Ironically, we have wanted to destroy the very same thing that, according to the Bible, we created with our original sin.

St. George is depicted as wolf-headed in this icon.

Saints and Wolves

With the growth of Christianity, early pagan beliefs were assimilated into the Bible's teachings, survived as folktales, or were attributed to the devil's cult. All over Europe, the positive aspects of pre-Christian wolf cults were suppressed.

In some cases the wolf gods were woven into Christian belief. For example, the Eastern European Saint George who is the wolf's patron is thought to have been a Christianized wolf god.

- One tale tells of St. George and his wolf companion, Lisun: A poor man watched St. George feed his sheep. When the saint was finished, he shared an extra loaf of bread with the hungry man. The loaf was magical, and turned out to be inexhaustible. The poor man's rich brother desired such a loaf himself, and went to St. George. This time, however, there was no extra loaf. St. George fed the rich man to the wolf.

- In Europe, it was said that St. Peter and his agents created wolves to punish those who, by eating meat, failed to properly observe his June 29th feast.

- A wolf was said to have guarded the severed head of the Anglo-Saxon king St. Edmund: "There lay the grey wolf who watched over that head, and had the head clasped between his two paws. The wolf was greedy and hungry, but because of God, he dared not eat the head, but protected it against animals. The people were astonished at the wolf's guardianship, and carried home with them the holy head, thanking almighty God for all His miracles. The wolf followed along with the head, as if he was tame, until they came to the settlement, and then the wolf turned back to the woods."[17]

- St. Francis tamed a vicious, bloodthirsty wolf by feeding it and treating it with kindness.

- On the eve of St. Andrew's Feast, villagers entered the woods howling to wolves through a clay pot, and fed them meat in an attempt to mitigate their behavior toward humanity.

- An eighteenth-century Greek icon represents St. Christopher wolf-headed, dressed as a soldier (reminiscent of the Egyptian wolf god Upuaut) in a red cloak, armed with a shield and spear, and accompanied by Archdeacon Stephanos.

- In ancient Hebraic legend, the Lord was said to have sent a plague of wolves to the Egyptians as punishment.

- St. Maedoc provided a feast for a pack of wolves.

- St. Hervé, who was blind, was led by a wolf.

A representation of a priest teaching a wolf the alphabet, from a twelfth-century frieze in Freiburg Cathedral, Germany. According to the Christian tale, once they had gotten as far as "c," the priest asked the wolf what he thought it might spell. "Lamb," declared the wolf. He was beaten for not allowing his thoughts to rise higher than the level of his stomach.

An illustration of the wolf from a medieval manuscript in the British Sloane collection. The animal is biting its paw as "punishment" because it made a sound while it was stalking sheep.

Science, Religion, and Magic

Just as interesting as the mythology surrounding the wolf are the scientific texts and encyclopedias dating from the Middle Ages. The information offered about wolves comprises little knowledge and a great deal of folklore. One text claims that the intelligence of the wolf increases and decreases along with the size of the moon. Another claims that wolves are the devil's hounds. The sixteenth-century *Aberdeen Bestiary* suggests that upon meeting a wolf, one should take off one's clothes, trample them underfoot, and beat two stones together—supposedly an effective deterrent. The Aberdeen also claims that the female wolf will whelp only while it is thundering and at no other time.

It is easy to find humor in these and other ancient beliefs about the wolf, but these texts shaped common opinion of the animal. The church controlled most book publications and nearly all types of learning, from illuminated manuscripts to the texts of the late Middle Ages, and few people were encouraged to learn the unbiased truth about wolves. Thus the largely negative folklore prospered and grew. According to nature writer Barry Lopez, author of *Of Wolves and Men*, the

first truly unbiased text about wolves—Adolph Murie's *The Wolves of Mt. McKinley*—was published in 1944. Before that, the texts that passed for scientific truth were filled with superstition.

Edward Topsell's sixteenth-century work *A Historie of Foure-Footed Beastes* is typical of contemporary and earlier texts of natural history. Excerpts from this text provide an understanding of the fallacy that was spread as scientific fact:

- "At the sight of a sheep the wolf makes an extraordinary noise with his foot, whereby he calls the sheep unto him. Standing amazed at the noise, a sheep falls into his mouth and is devoured."
- "Some writers say that if a wolf sees a man first, the man becomes silent and cannot speak, but if the man sees the wolf first, the wolf is silent and cannot cry. Although these things are reported by Plato and some other authors, I rather believe them to be fabulous than true."
- "Wolves are enemies to all and take special revenge against them that harm them. Some writers say that, when many wolves have obtained a

prey, they do equally divide it among them all, but whether this is true or not I cannot tell. Rather I think the contrary, because they are insatiable and never think they have enough."

"When wolves are in peril, they are extremely fearful, astonished, and afraid. When they are shut up, they seem harmless. This argues the baseness of their mind, which is subtle, cowardly, and treacherous, daring to do nothing but for the belly, and not then but upon singular advantage."

"Their eyes are yellow, black and very bright, sending forth beams like fire, and carrying in them apparent tokens of wrath and malice; and for this cause, it is said that they see better in the night than in the day."

"Some people are of the opinion that when wolves are old they grow weary of their lives and therefore come into cities and villages, offering themselves to be killed by men. But this is a fable."

Topsell relates the tale of a woman who panicked so intensely when a wolf wandered into her house that she fled instantly, shutting her children in the house with the wolf. Upon finding her husband and returning to the house, "The man entered hastily indoors, longing to save and deliver his poor infants. When he came in he found all well. The wolf was in worse case, for it stood like a stock without sense, astonished, amazed, and daunted. It was not able to run away and stood as if offering itself to be destroyed."

Representation of wolves from the Hortus Sanitatis *by Jean de Cuba. Editions of Ph. Le Noir, 1539.*

95

Wolves' Dark Ages

Respect for wolves all but disappeared once people began to rely on domesticated animals for food. Now a predator's caution was viewed as cowardice, conservation of energy was viewed as laziness, and the eating of huge amounts of food to guard against periods of scarcity was viewed as voracious gluttony. Even the respect the wolf had gained as a patron of warrior societies lost its importance as humans' close relationship with nature faded.

It is interesting to note that the push toward civilization brought about this dramatic turn in our perception of nature. This change in attitude is represented in simple things, like the word *savage*, which is derived from *silva*, meaning woods or forest. Thus, a savage is someone who comes from the woods. The fear of the woods, and of the people and animals that lived there, might have been born of the fact that the villages of the time were not as far removed from the savage lifestyle as their residents would have liked. Fields and villages could turn back to the wild after only a small period of neglect. An example is Perugia, Italy's, return to wildness in the late 1400s due to the violence of the ongoing feuds between the Baglioni and Oddi families. Houses were flattened, the land went untilled, peasants degenerated into plundering, murdering savages, and the bushes were peopled by stags and by wolves that fed on the flesh of the slain. This slim line between chaos and civilization is what the people—especially those in power—feared the most. To widen that gap, they chose to destroy elements of nature.

"Now that we are deprived of so great a benefit we dare not have regard to our own merits, but we fear rather lest, as a result of our sins, we should be exposed to the teeth of wolves: for the world, which lieth in evil, seeks to overthrow that which is just and holy, rather than to build up that which is deserving of veneration. And the devil, who is the enemy of the human race, when he sees that anyone is leading a specially devout and religious life, endeavors the more to create obstacles so that he may destroy what is holy, and may by crafty persuasion and wicked endeavor take it away so that it be not imitated by others."
—Bishop Rimbert, ninth-century missionary, Life of Anskar, the Apostle of the North, 801–865[18]

Notes, Section 2

1. See Aristotle's *Historia Animalium* and Pliny the Elder's *Historia Naturalis*, Barry Lopez *Of Wolves and Men*, 219.

2. Hall, Roberta L. and Sharp, Henry S. *Wolf and Man: Evolution in Parallel.* New York: Academic Press, 1978.

3. Shinto nature worship was formed from native folk beliefs in A.D. 500 or earlier.

4. Saxo Grammaticus, *The Danish History Books*, vol. I. A record of Scandinavian myth and folklore compiled in the Middle Ages.

5. Snorri Sturlasson, *Heimskringla*: "King Olaf Trygvason's Saga: Part II," sunsite.berkeley.edu/OMACL/Heimskringla.

6. Euripides, *Rhesos*, trans. Malcolm Smith, *Mythical and Fabulous Creatures*, Connecticut: Greenwood Press, 1987.

7. Unknown, *Avesta*, trans. L.H. Mills, www.avesta.org.

8. Reverend John Bachelor, FRGS, *The Ainu and Their Folklore* (London: The Religious Tract Society, 1901).

9. Edward Topsell, *A Historie of Foure-Footed Beastes* (London: printed by William Iaggard, 1607).

10. The *Avesta* is a collection of prophesies and scriptures, the oldest of which is from 600 B.C. www.avesta.org/zcomet.html.

11. Unknown, *Aberdeen Bestiary*, trans. Colin McLaren and Aberdeen University Library, www.clues.abdn.ac.uk, 1995. The name of this work is derived from Aberdeen College in South England, where the bestiary was kept.

12. E. A. Wallis Budge, *The Gods of the Egyptians*, vol. ii (London: Methuen & Company, 1904), 264.

13. Plato, *Phaedo*, trans. Benjamin Jowett, www.classics.mit.edu/Plato/Phaedo.sum.html.

14. Bruno Bettelheim, "Feral Children and Autistic Children," *American Journal of Sociology* 64, no. 5 (March 1959): 455–67.

15. See David Meeh, *The Wolf: The Ecology and Behavior of an Endangered Species* (New York: American Museum of Natural History, 1970 294-5) and Barry Lopez, *Of Wolves and Men* (New York: Charles Scribner's Sons, 1978 245-7).

16. R. A. Marchant, *Man and Beast* (London: G. Bell and Sons Ltd., 1966).

17. *Sweet's Anglo-Saxon Primer*, 9th ed., trans. Kenneth Cutler, Oxford: Oxford University Press 1961, 8 ff, www.fordham.edu Medieval Sourcebook: The Martyrdom of St Edmund, King of East Anglia, before 870.

18. Bishop Rimbert, *Life of Anskar, the Apostle of the North*, 801–865, trans. Charles H. Robinson, www.fordham.edu. Medieval Sourcebook.

Stained glass depicting the devil represented as a wolf, from Notre Dame de Quéménéven

A Chronology of Wolves and Humans

Myth and history are intricately woven together. Stories and beliefs about wolves have affected and in some cases even provoked our interactions with the animal. For example, a Swedish raiding party that garners strength and courage from wearing wolf skins attacks an English village sometime in the ninth century. The frenzy and cruelty of the attack influences tales told long into the future. A century later a man who grew up with tales of a dreadful "wolf" attack on the village may have an intensely negative attitude toward the animal and will relentlessly hunt, trap, torture, and kill it.

Wolves lived in North America for millions of years before the continent was inhabited by humans.

Those who have limited contact with wolves, and thus no real understanding of the animals, are most influenced by the stories they have been told and the beliefs that have been handed down through generations. We interpret the wolf's behavior through a filter determined by how, where, and when we were raised. Someone from Rwanda who has never seen or heard of a wolf will read its behavior differently than someone from France who grew up with terrifying stories of werewolves. In earlier times, however, our understanding of the animal was based on direct interaction with wolves. The wolf was considered our equal.

Our ancestors had a close understanding of wolves and their ways. Like wolves, they killed to eat, and death was part of everyday life. They were killed by the animals they hunted, by other tribes with whom they had territorial skirmishes, and by diseases for which they had no cure. These people understood the challenges and uncertainties of living in the wild: their every action was part of an effort to survive another day. Gradually, by developing hunting tools and building shelters, we were able to insulate ourselves from the severity of life in the wilderness. We cleared forests and built roads, removing anything that humbled us or barred our course toward civilization.

Eventually, we could no longer relate to predators that lived as we had once lived. We were shocked to see how wolves kill and eat their prey. Human weapons are quick and efficient, unlike wolves' teeth, which make for a bloody, prolonged death. Worst of all to domesticated minds, this predator begins to eat its prey while it is still kicking and struggling. However, wolves have no other choice; this is what they must do to survive. Once we forgot these realities of life in the wild, we began to see wolves as immoral, cowardly pests—competition for wild game, a threat to livestock, and an obstacle to civilization.

Over time, our changing perceptions have dramatically affected the wolf and its opportunity to survive.

Depictions of wolves on Saami drums.

The Chronicle of Wolves

Any chronology of our relationship with the wolf sketches out our changing views—positive and negative—and their impact on the animals' existence. Unfortunately there are large historical gaps where little is known of wolf-human relations except what has survived in artifacts and mythology. The availability of information—rich in some areas, scarce in others—has affected the character of the timeline below, which is intended to provide as full a view as possible of a changing relationship.

ORIGINS: 54,000,000–6000 B.C.

The canid family originated in North America thirty-eight to fifty-four million years ago. Between ten and fifteen million years ago, the *Canidae* line began to branch off and develop wolves, dire wolves, coyotes, jackals, foxes, and others. The ancestors of modern-day wolves evolved from small (approximately thirty-pound) canids until one to two million years ago, when they reached much the size they are today. These wolves, which are closer genetically to the red than to the gray wolf, migrated to Eurasia over the Siberian land bridge from their ancestral home in North America between six and eight hundred thousand years ago. This is when the first interaction between wolves and hominids is believed to have occurred. Three hundred thousand years ago, the gray wolf developed in Europe and a subspecies (believed to be *Canis lupus nublius*) returned from the Eurasian continent to North America via the resurfacing land bridge. Hundreds of thousands of years after wolves had developed into their present form, the first traces of *Homo sapiens* (dating from about 250,000 years ago) appeared in Africa. Anatomically modern humans did not develop until 150,000 years later.

A relatively peaceful relationship between wolves and hominids lasted for hundreds of thousands of years. Before humans developed long-distance hunting tools such as the bow and arrow, wolves and humans hunted in the same way. Ancient North American and Indo-European oral histories even give the wolf credit for teaching humans how to hunt. Humans sometimes

Four petroglyphs—from top to bottom, Egyptian, Native American, Siberian, and Asian Minor—that depict the wolf.

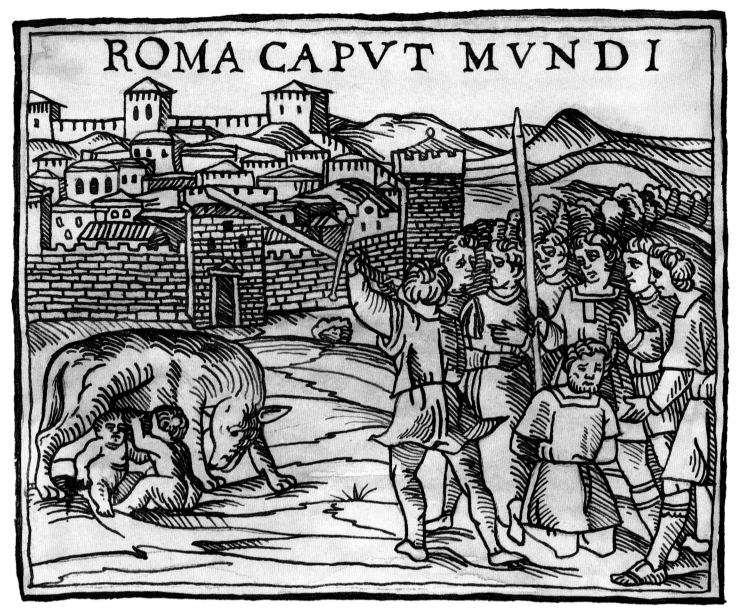

ROMA CAPVT MVNDI

Romulus and Remus, legendary founders of the city of Rome, suckling the she-wolf. Wood engraving from Roman History *by Tite Live, 1520.*

killed wolves for pelts, for ceremonial use, or even for food, but very rarely did they kill out of fear.

15000–10000 B.C.: The domestic dog was bred from wolves in the Middle East. Skeletal remains in other regions suggest that multiple domestication attempts occurred in unassociated cultures, implying that domestication was inevitable. A recent genetic study headed by Robert Wayne at UCLA has brought into question the widely accepted date of domestication, placing it instead at 100,000 B.C., which would explain the existing evidence of wolf bones in association with early human remains.[1] These early domestications may have been overlooked until recently because the skeletal structure of tame wolves was indistinguishable from that of wild wolves.

14000-10000 B.C.: The wolf appeared early in the birth of art. The earliest known depiction of a wolf is in the Font de Gaume cave in Dordogne, France. It is significant in that it is one of only two depictions of predators, and that the wolf is portrayed much as were prey species at that time: benign, fat, and with thin legs. One reason for this may be that the wolf was considered food by these people. Wolves were eaten in ancient China. Native Americans were known to eat wolves from time to time, and American explorers in the 1700s ate wolves in desperate times.

13000–12000 B.C.: The Paleo-Indians crossed the Beringia to North America, where the wolf had already been living for millions of years. Early dogs are believed to have accompanied these first settlers of North America. It is ironic that this early alliance of wolf and man created the first of many domestications of wild animals, ultimately producing livestock that would reshape our perception of wolves from respected equals into hated enemies.

Around 12000 B.C. the shift to permanent settlements and the clearing of wild lands around such settlements in the Levant (the coastal strip of Syria, Libya, and Israel) signaled the beginning of a move away from the wild.

10590 B.C.: In an engraved bone piece from Ariége, France, two wolves are depicted nose to nose. The great care taken in rendering the details of the wolves' features exhibits a certain respect and fascination. This piece of bone could have served as a physical representation of the wolf's strength. Humans attributed the wolf's hunting skills to magic and felt that carrying a piece of the animal's spirit as a fetish was one way to acquire that magic. The reverence for nature so clear in our ancestors' art gives us some insight into the nature religions, which prescribed that all things animate and inanimate had spirits and commanded respect.

8000 B.C.: The first signs of domestic donkeys, sheep, goats, and pigs marked the continuing push toward civilization.

6000 B.C.: An estimated twenty million wolves roamed throughout regions in the Eurasian, North American, and African continents, inhabiting every ecosystem that could sustain the animal.

CHANGING TIMES: 5000 B.C.–1700 A.D.

5000–3500 B.C.: Tripolitan painted ware depicted the wolf protecting crops as a fertility god.

3200–2700 B.C.: The wolf was revered in Egypt as the god of the underworld. However, this admiration of wolves did not last. When ethical religions began to take a strong hold in many cultures, the rift between man and nature widened.

In 622 B.C. the writing of the Old Testament began. The leaders of these ethical religions (which include Christianity and Zoroastrianism) projected human morals upon the wolf, and the animal was misunderstood and eventually hated. In the same century, Aesop's fables used the wolf as a symbol to teach morals and portrayed wolves as selfish, corrupt, immoral, and foolish.

By 600 B.C. the earliest known wolf bounty had been offered in Athens, Greece: five drachmas (the value of an ox) for a male and one drachma (the value of a sheep) for a female. Because the land was more suitable for pasture than for planting, the wolf had come to be considered destructive to the people's wealth.

600 B.C.: Iranian doctrines claimed that the evil Ahriman (the Zoroastrian devil) created the wolf.

400 B.C.: The earliest records of the tale of Romulus and Remus indicate that the wolf was still regarded as a fertility god at that time. These legendary founders of ancient Rome were said to have been born of and raised by a wild wolf.

"Homo homini lupus." (Man is, to man, a wolf.)
—Ciliades, Diffidentia[2]

Domestic Livestock and Depredation

Owners of domestic livestock often believe that their livelihood cannot survive in the presence of wolves. This conflict is the primary reason that world wolf populations have been so drastically reduced—farmers' bounties and government-hired predator control agents have had a devastating effect. However, history suggests that wolves and livestock can coexist, and wolf kills should not have to be a major concern of livestock owners. In Minnesota, where there are 1,700 wolves and 16,000 sheep, a twenty-year study reported that fewer than half a percent of the state's sheep and cattle are killed by wolves per year.[3] In Spain, arguably the country with the largest conflict between wolves and domestic livestock, it is estimated that depredation accounts for the loss of 2.5 percent of the total value of the livestock industry.[4] A much higher percentage of livestock dies due to each of the following individual causes: diseases, poisonous plants, poor husbandry practices, weather, and motor vehicles. Since wolves are such eager scavengers, deaths are often unfairly attributed to wolves when livestock die of natural causes. Wild dogs, of which there is a large population in Spain, have historically been notorious culprits in livestock losses, though in many cases wolves were and continue to be blamed.

Domestic dogs may be at risk in wolf territory. Because of their incessant barking, which wolves perceive as a threat, small and medium-sized dogs are in the most danger. Though these attacks are relatively uncommon, they do occur. In Sweden, loss of hunting dogs is one of the most feared results of a larger wolf population.

It is surprising that wolves do not attack livestock more frequently, since domestic animals are fatter, more plentiful, and easier to kill than wild prey. Domestic animals even entice wolves to attack by panicking in their presence. Wild prey will panic most noticeably when weakened, and wolves have learned that animals that react this way are easier to kill. These factors suggest that livestock should be preferred prey.

One of the reasons wolves avoid killing livestock is that adult wolves rarely start hunting new kinds of prey. When Fish and Wildlife Service agents brought in two bighorn sheep carcasses to feed orphaned wolf pups in the Ninemile Valley, Montana, "The pups were used to whitetails and wouldn't touch the sheep. They circled them repeatedly, and only nibbled on a small portion near one of the shoulders. . . . If they haven't seen their parents eat it—if they haven't developed a taste for it within the pack's confines—chances are fair they won't develop a taste for it out of the blue. The implications with regards to cattle depredation are obvious."[5]

However, when wolves grow old, or if wild prey is unavailable, wolves can develop the habit of killing livestock. Some of the more horrific killings of domestic stock were attributed to the last remaining wild wolves of the southwestern United States in the late 1800s. The reputations of these wolves were of nearly mythic proportions.

Decoration on a stone lintel from Saint-Pierre de Vieux, Lyon, France.

The legends were often so embellished that when the wolves were finally killed and displayed in town, people were invariably disappointed that they were so much smaller than expected, and didn't look a bit like the vicious beasts that the townspeople had envisioned. These remaining wolves were often lone wolves who learned to avoid traps and poison by eating only from fresh kills and to avoid hunters by traveling all over their range. In the most extreme case, one wolf reportedly killed fifty thousand dollars' worth of livestock, often eating only a small amount or nothing at all. These rare but memorable occurrences are what people choose to recollect when it is proposed that wolves be reintroduced into territory occupied by domestic stock.

Historically, nomadic farming practices in which animals were given free range on predominantly public lands suffered the most from depredation by wolves. However, there are more effective ways to curb livestock losses than killing wolves. French shepherds have found that they can keep wolves away from their flocks by employing sheepdogs, shepherding more vigilantly, and using gas-powered noisemakers. In areas where electric fences are used, wolves and sheep have been able to live side by side with no occurrences of depredation. Many countries with populations of wolves and livestock have established funds that give out monetary redemption for livestock lost to wolves; in this way the cost is shared by wolf supporters and the hatred for wolves is lessened.

Lifestyle of the Shepherd

A recent study in Greece illustrates shepherds' current attitude towards wolves.[6] Greece's low density of natural prey and high density of livestock has caused wolves to inflict considerable damage upon domestic animals. This has created animosity towards the predator: 72 percent of wolf killings by humans were a result of attacks or believed attacks on domestic stock. Farmers cannot physically fight government regulations, poor weather, livestock diseases, poverty, or isolation, but they *can* fight the wolf. Thus, wolves have become a symbol of farmers' hardships. They are killed with vigor and their deaths are celebrated. Even to this day, the hunter is rewarded with money or animals.

It is interesting that older shepherds tend to have more respect for wolves, since the animal confirms their purpose and challenges their skills. This difference in attitude is exemplified in reports of livestock losses. Traditionally the loss of livestock to wolves was not reported because these losses were considered proof of the shepherd's failure. But currently, it is common to see angry shepherds in televised news complaining of wolf attacks.

"Savage berserks roaring mad,
And champions fierce in wolf-skins clad,
Howling like wolves; and clanking jar
Of many a mail-clad man of war.
Thus the foe came; but our brave king
Taught them to fly as fast again."

—Hornklofe, thirteenth-century
Scandinavian poet, describing
the battle at Hafnersfjord.[7]

About a Wolf: Image and text from a fifteen-page sensationalist newspaper printed by M. Buffet in Paris, 1587

A.D. 400–1500: In the Middle Ages, grave misconceptions about wolves were perpetuated by myths and fables that depicted wolves negatively and by bestiaries that were presented as scientific truth but were written to promote the morals of the church. The idea of werewolves arose from the widespread belief that wolves were the physical manifestation of the dark, primitive side of man. The Roman Church was able to manipulate believers into seeking out and killing both wolves and werewolves—that is, nonbelievers. Bounties, unlimited hunting seasons, and *grand battues*, or drives, in which the animals were driven toward and killed by armed men were arranged to rid the land of wolves. In 985, King Edgar of England accepted taxes paid in wolf heads and fines in wolf tongues, and demanded three thousand wolfskins a year from the King of Wales. After three years the tax was revoked, as there were no more wolves to be found. In 1487 the *Malleus Maleficarum* ("The Hammer of Witches") was published with the intention of refuting every objection to the belief in werewolves and proving that they were the devil's accomplices. This document also claimed that wolves were either agents of God sent to punish evil men or agents of the devil sent to torment the good.

617: According to Caesar Baronius, an ecclesiastical historian of the late 1500s, in this year a pack of wolves entered a monastery and attacked monks who were known to have heretical opinions. (This account was intended to attest not to the saintliness of wolves but rather to the vileness of the offenders, who were considered *worse* than wolves.) Similarly, wolves were said to have attacked members of the army of Francesco Maria, an Italian duke, who intended to ravage the holy house of Loreto.

1042–66: Edward the Confessor used the term "wolf" in written law in lieu of the word "criminal." To call "wolf's head" upon an outlaw meant that he could be morally and legally killed at any time, in any way, much as wolves were at the time. In medieval Europe, wolves were hung side by side with criminals on the gallows.

1162–1227: Genghis Khan, the Mongolian conqueror who united North China, Central Asia, Iran, and South Russia under his rule, claimed that he was born of a superior blue-gray wolf, which was itself sired by the sky.

1270: Those who did not believe in werewolves were denounced by the leaders of the Christian church as heretics, although in a sermon in 870 the archbishop of Mainz had stated in no uncertain terms that shapeshifting was merely a superstition.

1347–1351: When the bubonic plague struck Europe, killing more than twenty-five million people, wolves roamed the graveyards scavenging the unburied corpses and even unearthing the dead from shallow graves.

Early 1500s: The last wolves of England were killed.

1546: Construction of the Louvre museum began in Paris; the building was named after the wolves that roamed its grounds (*louve*: "she-wolf").[9]

1598–1600: A French magistrate sentenced six hundred citizens to death for being werewolves.

1600: The French court deemed werewolves to be heretics rather than supernatural beings. Three years later the French court declared lycanthropy to be an insane delusion.

1697: The first version of Charles Perrault's "Little Red Riding Hood" was published. This tale, and others such as "The Seven Little Goats [or Geese]," and "The Three Little Pigs," played upon children's

Detail of an engraving depicting Peter Stubb's fate in Cologne, France, as a "convicted" werewolf.

"Wolf-coats they call them, that in battle
Bellow into bloody shields.
They wear wolves' hides when they
come into the fight,
And clash their weapons together."
—Hornklofe, "Raven Song."[10]

fears of monsters preying on the weak and defenseless. Again the wolf was used as a metaphor for the ever-lurking inner beast in humans: rather than frightening children away from real wolves, the fables encouraged safe and proper behavior by associating strangers with wolves. To this day, by the age of three a child has learned of the supposedly terrible nature of wolves through these fables.

1700s: In Europe, wolves had successfully been rooted out of the most densely populated areas and were pushed farther and farther back into the remote wilderness. According to Carl Linné, an eighteenth-century Swedish scientist, wolves were seldom seen in middle and southern Sweden in the 1700s.

The last Scottish wolf was killed in 1743, and the last Irish wolf was killed in 1770. By 1800, with the exception of pockets of populations in remote wild lands, most of the wolves in Europe had been exterminated.

Detail of an illustration from a medieval manuscript depicting a wolf in the role of the snake in the Garden of Eden. Created by a German or Bohemian master, 1200.

"March 25, 1065, Good Friday about the second hour of the day,
just as they were leaving Kafar Sallam, they suddenly fell into the hands of the Arabs
who leaped on them like famished wolves on long-awaited prey.
They slaughtered the first pilgrims pitiably, tearing them to pieces."
—Annalist of Nieder-Altaich: The Great German Pilgrimage of 1064–65 [11]

RELATION
CURIEUSE,
VÉRITABLE ET REMARQUABLE,

"Curious, genuine and astonishing accounts…" A page from a sensationalist newspaper detailing attacks on humans by a ferocious animal in Périgord, France. Printed in August 1766 by d'Houry, Paris.

THE NEW WORLD: 1607–1700

1607: The British settled Jamestown. Early settlers from European cities found America to be a wilderness entirely foreign to them, and this strangeness engendered fear and misconceptions. In 1620, when the Pilgrims arrived at Plymouth Rock, they were shocked to find the land "infested" with wolves. Wolves had been extirpated in England over one hundred years earlier, and most settlers had encountered them only in myths, folklore, or scientific texts, all of which maligned the animal. Since the Bible depicted wolves as the embodiment of the devil, settlers sought to destroy them, to rid their new colony of all filth and evil. A minister describing the New World wrote, "Our greatest enemies are the wolves."

Though such hatred was common, not all men feared wolves. Settlers who lived in the colonies for some time knew that the wolf was not harmful to humans and tried to convince newcomers. Still, the myths gained in strength.

1625: Colonists in North America believed that they were losing a great deal of livestock to the wolf. The colonists commonly blamed all canine (fox, coyote,

"Is he a lamb? His skin
is surely lent him,
For he's inclined as
is a ravenous wolf."
—William Shakespeare,
Henry VI, 1590

and domestic dog) predation on the wolf. If a sheep died of disease and was scavenged by dogs, it was often reported as a wolf kill. Because domestic animals were imported by boat from Europe they were very valuable, and every livestock loss was tragic. In 1630 Massachusetts set a bounty on wolves. In 1648 all communities were urged by the Massachusetts General Assembly to acquire dogs to kill wolves. The flaw with this plan was that not all of the dogs were herding dogs; they often attacked the sheep themselves—although these attacks were frequently reported as wolf kills. By 1800, when wolves were but a memory in the original colonies, dogs were officially reported to be the chief cause of decline in the sheep market.

Deer became an important source of both food and clothing, and the settlers were in competition with the wolf again. So profitable was this new industry that "buck," an abbreviation of "buckskin," became a synonym for money. When deer herds and much of the other native prey in the colonies declined in number due to ceaseless human hunting (in one year thirty thousand deer were killed in North Carolina alone), wolves were believed responsible for the loss. In the eyes of the settlers, wolves stole not only clothing and food but also money.

Drastic plans were made to protect people from wolves. In 1717 one such proposal was to build an eight-mile-long, six-foot-high fence cutting off Cape Cod from the rest of the colonies to protect the peninsula from wolves. The project was abandoned only after it proved too expensive. Bounties were set, baits were laid, pits were dug, palisades were erected—anything to keep the wolf and wilderness at bay. A New York law from the late 1640s authorizing bounties clearly stated its goal that "the breed of Wolves may be wholly rooted out and extinguished."

WESTWARD EXPLORATION AND EXPANSION: 1740–1893

Mid-1700s: Explorers began to travel the American frontier and discovered "wolves without number" on the Great Plains. Some explorers claimed to have seen hundreds of wolves in one day (although these early explorers didn't differentiate between coyotes and wolves). Accustomed to following Native American hunters to scavenge any remains of their kills, the wolves also followed the frontier hunters. These wolves quickly finished off whatever carcasses the hunters left unattended, and when the frontiersmen returned to collect more meat from "their" carcass they cursed the wolves for leaving nothing but bones. The explorers of the American frontier were shocked at the wolves' brazenness.

Wolves annoyed frontiersmen further by running off with kettles, pans, hats, and other objects that captured the animals' curiosity. One wolf even made off with a prized leather saddle that it gently pulled out from beneath a pioneer's head as he slept.[12] In these early days of exploration wolves were rarely killed, since the animal was not a threat and ammunition was in short supply.

1780s: Wolves, bears, and most game animals were hunted out of existence in the eastern colonies by the late 1780s. Having heard from explorers about the rich land and game to be had on the Great Plains, the settlers turned westward. Wolf pelts became fashionable, and between 1780 and 1799 three hundred and thirty thousand wolves from eastern Canada, the Mississippi Valley, the Appalachian mountain range, and the Great Lakes region were killed for their pelts.

1800s: Expansion into the West forced pioneers and fur traders to share land and game with wolves. The enormous herds of bison were a virtual gold mine and hunters collected with gusto. Wolves soon learned to follow the sound of gunshots to feed on the vast numbers of carcasses that the fur traders left behind.

In the early 1800s the hunters killed wolves for sport and left them to rot, but around 1865 wolf fur became popular again and the animal became valuable. Between 1860 and 1880, professional wolf hunters or "wolfers" roamed the plains, killing bison, depositing strychnine in the carcasses, and then collecting the furs of the dead wolves. One wolfer claimed to have killed 120 wolves this way in one night. Strychnine was used generously in the American West to kill an extraordinary number of wolves and also millions of other animals. Stanley Young, a wolf hunter, wrote of the 1800s that "there was a sort of unwritten law of the range that no cowman would knowingly pass by a carcass of any kind without inserting in it a goodly amount of Strychnine sulfate, in the hope of killing one more wolf." This attempt to "tame" North America led to the deaths of an estimated five hundred million untargeted animals (raccoons, black-footed ferrets, red foxes, ravens, red-tailed hawks, bald eagles, eagles, ground squirrels, and wolverines, among others) as well as one to two million wolves.

1833: A rabid wolf wandered into a camp in western Wyoming and killed thirteen people. Although rabid wolves were uncommon, such occurrences fed the growing negativity and quickened the wolf's extirpation.

1872-1919: Yellowstone National Park and other national parks were set aside as nature preserves where wild game could be seen in its habitat. Park planners felt that to achieve this goal of a natural haven, all predators (with the exception of man) must be destroyed. Park rangers were employed by the government to shoot, trap, and poison wolves and other predators in Yellowstone, Glacier, McKinley/Denali, Rocky Mountain, Grand Canyon, Wind Cave, Mesa Verde, Mount Rainier, Yosemite, Sequoia, Crater Lake, and Zion. In addition, the U.S. government spent millions of dollars on wolf bounties to pay independent wolf hunters.

In hindsight, it is difficult to understand how it was acceptable to "preserve" nature not as it was found but rather as the sportsman would like it to be—to the sportsman, fewer predators meant more game and limitless hunting. The drawback to maintaining this hunter's paradise is that the land can

Canis lupus lycaon

Tall Tales

Frontiersmen used animal stories to boast of their own cunning, and exchanged wild tales about the intelligence of animals mainly as proof of their own prowess. Here is a comical legend: Surprised by a pack of wolves in the woods, a hunter escaped by climbing a tree. The wolves prowled about at the base of the tree for two hours and then left, leaving one wolf to guard the hunter. After half an hour the pack returned—with a beaver to fell the tree.

Fearing Wolves

Humans fear the snarling child-killer of storybooks. Real wolves have many of the qualities humans have assigned to mythical monsters: long teeth, intense eyes, and a tendency to lurk in the shadows.

All over the world, people believe that the wolf is dangerous. Accounts of wolves attacking humans flood history books, folktales, and oral histories. The sheer number of these reports seems to affirm that wolves really are dangerous to humans. However, those who have close contact with wolves, both captive and wild, claim that there is no need for humans to fear this animal. In remote places where the wolf has not been persecuted, it will approach humans with simple curiosity, posing no threat. Traditionally, Native American people have expressed no fear of the animal. Explorers and trappers of the early 1800s wrote with great surprise of the wolf's timidity. U.S. Colonel Richard Irving Dodge wrote that wolves were such cowards that one alone did not possess enough courage to attack a sheep.[13] According to a study of European accounts of wolf attacks , not a single report from 1815 to 1965 could be authenticated.[14] Another study tracked down every report of wolf attacks from 1923 to 1936. All of them were found to be either fictional or extremely exagger-

ated.[15] In some cases a report of wolves killing humans turned out to be a human attack (since *wolf* can be a synonym for *outlaw*); other accounts told of animals whose behavior proved that they were plagued with rabies (a rare disease in wild wolves). In Russia, the wolf has served as a scapegoat where political "disappearances" and "lost" children (who were purposely left in the forest) have traditionally been reported as wolf attacks. In other cases the "wolves" were proven to be wolf–dog hybrids. The latter explanation was found to be the case in one of the more famous accounts of wolf attacks, the story of the Beast of Gévaudan.

Between the years of 1764 and 1766 two animals killed sixty-four people and attacked more than one hundred domestic animals in the region of Gévaudan, France. When the "wolves" were finally captured and killed, descriptions of them were recorded and their skulls were measured. According to measurements in the existing documents, scientists now believe that these enormous animals (approximately 140 pounds each) were wolf-dog hybrids.

Healthy wild wolves simply do not prey upon humans. Even when the wolf's offspring, food, or life is in danger, the animal is unlikely to act aggressively toward humans. Wolves by nature retreat when approached. Biologist David Mech has frightened large packs away from freshly killed prey simply by walking toward them. In one such instance two large wolves came bounding back toward the carcass: "I immediately drew my revolver, preparing to fire above them. But I never needed to. At my very first movement the wolves halted abruptly, turned and fled back to the pack. Evidently the smell of the fresh carcass had overcome my own odor, and the wolves had not realized that I was still there. When suddenly reminded, they departed quickly."[16] Similarly, when naturalist Adolph Murie stole a pup from a wolf den, the parents did no more than bark and howl in protest.[17] In his *Wolves of Mt. McKinley*, Murie claims that two hikers caught a wolf pup by the tail when the mother was only 150 yards away. Though she barked she made no attempt to attack.

Often when wolves are unable to flee from danger they do not seem to put up much of a defense toward humans. At worst, they will occasionally growl and snarl when their dens or their lives are threatened. Researchers who regularly trap and study wolves tranquilize them—not for their own safety, but to avoid traumatizing the animals. European sheep-herders have traditionally carried only a cane to ward off wolves.

At their most vulnerable, wolves are often extremely submissive. One trapper who habitually hunted wolves used a forked stick to keep a trapped wolf's head to the ground as he broke its neck with his hands. Another account tells of a wolf that, upon seeing its captor approach, raised its trapped paw and whined piteously. All of this indicates that the wolf is not aggressive toward humans.

Some of the fear humans have of wolves can be attributed to the wolf's method of communication, which may seem excessively aggressive.

The Danger of "Fearless" Wolves

In Algonquin Park, Canada, there have recently been disturbing incidents of fearless wolves harming humans. None of these attacks have been fatal, but they do indicate that wolves that consistently display fearless behavior could pose a threat to humans. In one 1996 case, a twelve-year-old boy was pulled several feet in his sleeping bag and bitten on the face by a wolf. Two years later, a wolf seized a nineteen-month-old boy by the ribcage and tossed him three feet. The boy's mother ran to pick up her son while the boy's father and other campers frightened the wolf away. Such incidents are difficult to understand. If these wolves regarded the children as prey, they would surely have inflicted much more harm. The wolves may have simply been investigating. However, the Algonquin Park wolves were clearly too curious for human safety. All of the wolves involved in these incidents were noted early on for their unusual behavior. The only way to prevent further occurrences is to make efforts to teach such wolves to avoid humans.

Only in recent times has extensive research been undertaken on wolf populations outside of North America. In most countries the animal has been considered a pest, so wolf research has received little interest. The wolf depicted here is Canis lupus pallipes, *which lives in India, Iraq, Israel, Turkey, and Saudi Arabia.*

only sustain a finite number of herbivores, and predators help keep herds balanced by killing the weaker individuals. Native Americans, who had a unique understanding of predator-prey relations, took the concept further, believing that if all wolves were killed, the prey population would actually decline.

1873–93: At the same time bison were hunted nearly to extinction, the profession of wolfing fell into decline, and a new, profitable enterprise began on the Great Plains. Raising livestock on the open range became a widespread practice, and by 1885, twenty million cattle overran the plains. These animals were herded up only twice a year—once in spring to brand new calves and again in the fall to sell them; otherwise they were completely free to roam on public land. Since the population of wild prey was so drastically depleted, many wolves were now forced to subsist on cattle.

Initially profit was so high that when wolves took 5 percent of the cattle herd, it was overlooked. A string of financially catastrophic events would soon change that attitude. The price of calves dropped drastically in 1885; drought killed hundreds of thousands of cattle in 1887; free grazing on public land was discontinued; and another three-year drought caused nationwide financial panic. Livestock owners were left reeling.

The wolf bounty had been repealed in 1890, but now that ranchers leased land from the government they insisted that it should be free of predators. By inflating the numbers of livestock lost to wolves, ranchers tried to persuade the government that the animal needed to be eradicated. The Wyoming State legislature was convinced to allocate more money to wolf bounties than to the state university for the next seven years. In Montana, overreported losses of cattle to wolves convinced the legislature to reinstate the wolf bounty in 1893. Eventually these bounties were so high that hunters sought out wolves in more and more remote areas, and wolves were trapped and poisoned with renewed vigor.

Early 1900s: The U.S. government hired its own wolf killers to protect cattle and wild game. At this point a few people began to speak in defense of wolves. People like Ernest Thompson Seton circulated stories that were "mostly" true, depicting the wolf as a martyr but also as a ravenous murderer. Captain W. R. Kennedy wrote of the Newfoundland wolf (now extinct), vilified for its alleged attacks on local livestock, that

> wolves are not, in my opinion, so numerous as many suppose. . . . I do not believe they do half as much harm as they are credited with, and certainly not as much as the packs of half-wild, half-starved curs which infest the country. If government were to give a reward for every one of these brutes which was shot, it would be more to the purpose. They are without a doubt the curse of the country; no farmer can keep either sheep or cattle for fear of them. The settlers keep them for hauling lumber. . . . These brutal dogs are not fed, but they are left to get their own living.[18]

At this time, newspapers reported disturbing stories of wolves attacking humans: a skeleton of a logger was said to have been found still choking the skeleton of a wolf; mailmen were killed and eaten by wolves that left only bloody hands and feet. So many outrageous tales of killer wolves were reported that James Curran, the editor of the Sault Ste. Marie, Ontario, *Daily Star*, offered a prize of one hundred dollars to anyone who could prove that he or she had been attacked. Fourteen years after the offer was made, the paper reported that "the prize is still safe in the editor's cash box."

1905: Montana passed a bill requiring veterinarians to infect wolves with mange. This continued for eleven years in spite of the program's cruelty, and despite the spread of the disease to domestic stock and wild animals.

The hatred of wolves was so widespread and the misunderstandings of the species were so severe that even early-twentieth-century conservationist-zoologist William Hornaday said of wolves, "There is no depth of meanness, treachery, or cruelty to which they do not cheerfully descend. They are the only animals on earth which make a regular practice of killing and devouring their wounded companions, and eating their own dead."[19]

1914–1915: The outbreak of World War I and an epidemic of rabies convinced the government to allocate $125,000 for wolf and coyote destruction. The theory was that killing these animals would protect domestic stock, which would feed the allied forces.

1920s: Predator hunters hired by the U.S. government reached a peak number of five hundred. The utopia of a world without predators proved to be a false vision: as America's deer population grew, the deer began to destroy their own habitat.

1929: Predator extermination, now called "control," was initiated in Alaska to preserve big game, although the decline of wild game was actually caused by harsh winters and human hunting. The excuses made to kill wolves were transparent; Alaska's wolf control laws were created to protect the interests of sport hunters, who were a source of substantial revenue for local businesses. In 1931 Mt. McKinley's rangers were ordered to kill wolves on sight.

1940s: Despite noted biologist Adolph Murie's extensive study on wolf-prey ecology, which determined that wolves were not the cause of the decline in wild game,[20] sportsmen pushed for large-scale eradication of wolves in Alaska in order to protect wild game. Even the U.S. Fish and Wildlife Service (USFWS) Division of Information chief stated that "in man's scheme of things, at least, the wolf has no place." In Alaska, the wolf bounty was raised from $30 to $50, and $104,000 in additional federal funding was provided to hire nine more wolf-control agents in order to save both nonnative reindeer and wild game from certain eradication by "bloodthirsty" wolves. Among the methods of wolf control, airborne hunting (introduced in 1952) and poison were used extensively. With these combined efforts, by 1958 two thousand wolves had been killed in Alaska.

Wolves as Outlaws

In the late nineteenth century, as the great United States attack on wolves slackened, certain individual animals became legendary for their uncanny evasion of traps and poison. Ranchers touted these wolves as devious criminals that sought revenge against humans. A bounty of one thousand dollars was placed on "Lobo," one of these legendary wolves. He and his pack were heavily hunted for five years in Currumpaw Valley, New Mexico, and by the time Ernest Thompson Seton offered his services to rid the ranch of the wolf, Lobo's pack had killed more than two thousand cattle. This clever and elusive wolf amazed Seton, a popular writer of nature stories. He recorded his dedicated pursuit of the Currumpaw wolf and discovered a newfound respect for the animal. Subsequently, he used his 1894 account *Lobo, King of the Currumpaw* as an argument for the nobility of the species, and as an appeal to halt their destruction.

Over a period of four months, Seton went to great lengths to make the traps and poison he laid out for Lobo impossible to detect. He prepared bait made from cheese and kidney fat while wearing gloves

"steeped in the hot blood of a heifer" to avoid tainting the bait with human odor. After carefully inserting odorless strychnine/cyanide capsules into four pieces of bait which he had cut with a bone knife, Seton placed them in a rawhide bag rubbed all over with blood. On horseback, he dragged this bag for ten miles, then dropped a lump of bait every quarter mile.

The next day, Seton followed the pack's tracks leading to the first bait, which had been taken. Following the trail Seton found that the second and third baits had also been taken. But Lobo had carried them in his mouth and "dropped them all when he came to the fourth. There he had scattered filth all over them to express his utter contempt for all my stratagems." Seton's steel wolf traps were treated and laid out with similar care, and in one case Lobo actually backtracked his way out of a field of buried traps, "carefully putting each paw in its old track." Lobo kept himself and his pack safe by avoiding the traps and eating only freshly killed meat.

Eventually, temptation brought Lobo's mate, Blanca, directly into a well-placed trap. "We drew a lasso over the neck of the doomed wolf and strained our horses in opposite directions until the blood burst from her mouth, her eyes glazed, her limbs stiffened and then fell limp." Blanca's death was typical of the treatment which wolves received at the hands of men who believed they were taming the wilderness. Our past is full of such hunters who tortured and mutilated wolves with unnerving zeal.

Lobo searched for Blanca and "when he reached the spot where his mate had died he seemed to know what had happened and his wailing was piteous to hear." Seton renewed his efforts to ensnare Blanca's cunning mate by making tracks toward a nest of traps with her severed paw. Upon following his mate's familiar scent Lobo walked right into the traps he had previously gone to such great lengths to avoid: "As soon as he was bound he made no further resistance and uttered no sound. . . . I put meat and water beside him but he paid no heed. He did not even move a muscle when I touched him, but turned his head away, gazing past me down the canyon to the open plains—the kingdom where he had so long hunted and triumphed. Thus he lay until sundown."

Though Seton has been criticized for adding fictional drama to his writings, what we know about the bonds between pack members makes it difficult to respond to this account with detachment.

It is said that a lion shorn of his strength,
an eagle robbed of his freedom and a dove
bereft of his mate will die of a broken heart.
Who will say that this grim bandit could
bear the loss of all three? This only I know:
When the morning came he was lying just
as I left him; but his spirit was gone—the
king-wolf was dead. A cowboy helped me
carry him into the shed where the remains
of Blanca lay. As we placed Lobo beside her,
the cattleman looked down at him and said,
'There—you would come to her; now you
are together again.'[21]

Intolerance Toward Wolves

Not only have humans set out to eliminate wolves, at times they have also taken satisfaction in torturing them. This cruel expression of hatred for another species has been justified by the Machiavellian theory wherein the ends justify the means: killing wolves was man's duty to humankind, to civilization, and to the church. The 1920s slogan of one regional supervisor of the Predatory Animal and Rodent Control service (PARC) sums up the idea nicely: "Bring Them In Regardless of How."

The instances of cruelty to wolves are many:

- The Saamis—Scandinavian reindeer herders—sought out wolf dens and poked out wolf pups' eyes because they believed that this would convince the pack to leave the area, whereas killing the pups would cause the pack to seek revenge.

- Set guns were triggered by trip wires or baited. This contraption killed all kinds of animals, but when one decapitated a child in Long Island, New York, in 1650, set guns were banned to a radius half a mile outside of town and allowed to be set only at night.

- Hunters have trapped wolves and disabled them, releasing the animals with their Achilles tendons cut, their jaws wired shut, or their lower jaws sawed off. Unable to hunt or eat, sometimes even unable to move, these wolves died an excruciatingly slow death.

- In America in the 1800s people set thousands of acres on fire in attempts to rid the land of wolves, mistakenly destroying forests, crops, and even their own homes in the process.

- Adult wolves were killed and their trusting pups were removed from the den. Though it sickened them to do it, U.S. federal predator control agents strangled the pups.

- Wolves have been doused with gasoline and burned alive.

- In the early 1900s, wolves in America were infected with highly contagious mange and released in the hope of infecting pack members. A serious oversight became obvious when this disease spread to game species and livestock.

- In present-day Saudi Arabia, wolves are killed and hung from a tree or post with their eyes gouged out. This is believed to avert bad spirits.

Presently, relatively few wolves inhabit the earth—only about 1 percent of their estimated population in 6000 B.C. Since the Middle Ages, the idea has been propagated that humankind would be gentler and kinder without the influence of the wolf. But is the world so much better without wolves? Wolf hunter Elbert Bowman believed wolves to be "as cruel as man himself," but it is not the wolf that is to blame for

Trapped in 1929 near Gillham, Arkansas, this red wolf had its jaws wired shut and was tied to a stake. Such wolves either died of dehydration or were killed by dogs.

humankind's brutality. The hatred of wolves we have displayed has truly brought out the worst of human nature. On using poison to kill wolves, Ernest Thompson Seton wrote, "What right has man to inflict such horrible agony on fellow beings merely because they do a little damage to his material interests?" Vernon Bailey, the government hunter who recommended the wolf's eradication in areas containing domestic stock, said that though wolves were cruel killers they were "not half as cruel as we have been." Perhaps what humankind fears the most, and has been trying to kill by destroying the wolf, is the evil that exists within us.

*The Mexican wolf (Canis lupus baileyi) derives its sub-
species name from Vernon Bailey, a biologist for the U.S.
Department of Agriculture who was one of the most
outspoken proponents of the animal's destruction.*

1947–72: Canada still had a sizable wolf population,
although the country was making great efforts to
eliminate the animal. In Ontario, bounty hunters
managed to kill thirty-three thousand wolves in this
twenty-five-year period. In 1948, poison and traps
were set in Alberta as a campaign against rabies.
After eight years of poisoning, fifty-five hundred
wolves were killed. Only one was infected with rabies.

CHANGING PERCEPTIONS: 1940–2000

During World War II the wolf population grew in
Europe due to humans' shift of focus. After the war
ended, Europeans were again encouraged to kill
wolves by any means. In some countries, thousands
of wolves were killed annually. In Russia, for example,
62,700 wolves were killed in 1946 alone, and for the
next fifteen years, 40,000 to 50,000 wolves were
killed annually.

1950: Because of habitat destruction and relentless
hunting, the last wolves were eliminated from the
majority of western Europe (with the exception of
Italy and Spain). In North America, human settlement and persecution reduced the wolf population
by 95 percent.

1960: Popular opinion began to shift as interest in the
wolf grew. In 1967 the red wolf was declared an
endangered species. The population of *Canis rufus*
had been enormously reduced due to large-scale
extermination as well as the destruction of habitat
by land clearing and drainage projects, logging, min-
eral exploration, and road development. The small
number of wolves forced hybridization with coyotes,
further diminishing the true wolf population.

1966: Lin Piao, minister of defense of the People's
Republic of China, made a speech claiming that
"like a vicious wolf, [imperialism/fascism is] bully-
ing and enslaving various peoples, plundering their
wealth, encroaching upon their countries' sovereign-
ty, and interfering with their international affairs.
It is the most rabid aggressor in human history
and the most ferocious common enemy of the people of the world." Such symbolism in speeches,
stories, films, and other media is always scalding
to the wolf's reputation.

1971-72: The U.S. federal predator control program
was criticized for spending $110 million of public
money in a twenty-year period for the benefit of private agriculture. Aerial hunting (locating, pursuing,
and shooting wolves from airplanes), common in
Alaska, was banned for its cruelty in 1972.

1973: International protection of the wolf began with
the drafting of the *Manifesto of Wolf Conservation*. In
the United States the Endangered Species Act, created to protect habitats as well as animals, was passed.

Efforts continued to save the endangered red wolf, and
wild wolves were captured over the next seven years
with the goal of creating a captive breeding population.
From the four hundred wolflike animals caught, testing revealed that only seventeen were pure red wolves.
(Hybridization with coyotes had begun in the late
1800s when coyotes moved eastward and red wolves
took them as mates since their own species was vanish-
ing.) Of those seventeen pure red wolves, only fourteen
were successfully bred.

1974: The USFWS and Northern Michigan University attempted to introduce four wolves from Minnesota into Michigan's Upper Peninsula. Two wolves were shot and killed, a third was trapped, and a motorist struck the fourth.

As wolf researcher Dr. Félix Rodríguez de la Fuente mentioned in a 1975 meeting of wolf specialists in Stockholm, Count Mayalde of Spain once claimed that his was not a civilized country because it was a country in which wolves lived. But only a civilized country can live at peace with its wolves. A civilized country deals with its surrounding environment ethically, basing its conservation decisions on impartial science for the betterment of the whole, not for special-interest groups that have money and therefore power. Too commonly, biologists' results are swayed for fear of losing work. For example, when his studies in Algonquin Park, Canada, showed that trapping and logging seriously damaged the park's wolf population, John Theberge's career was threatened.[22] Upon recommending government action that would result in a loss of revenue for special interest groups, biologists have faced funding cuts, exclusion from their studies, and ruined reputations. In 1976, wildlife biologist Vic VanBallenberge was transferred from his position in the Alaskan Department of Fish and Game (ADFG) because he resisted orders to increase wolf-control research.[23] The biologist who replaced him killed every wolf within three thousand square miles with the intention of increasing the moose population. There was no effect on the moose. Unfortunately, conservation generally can't compete against the influence of politics. The ADFG, for example, earns several million dollars each year from licenses and big-game permits.

1976: The Mexican wolf (*Canis lupus baileyi*) was listed as an endangered species.

August 1979: The wolf was listed in Appendix II ("Strictly Protected Species") of the Bern Convention on the Conservation of European Wildlife and Natural Habitats. This listing allowed the wolf and its habitat full protection. However, the individual countries were responsible for enforcing the policy, and any participating country could obtain an exemption from the agreement to protect wolves.

1977–1980: The remaining wild Mexican wolves were captured in an effort to begin a captive breeding program of animals with the intention of eventually releasing wolves in the wild. Only five wolves were found, and Mexican wolves were declared extinct in the wild. By 1982 the USFWS had designed a recovery plan for Mexican wolves, though the entire population comprised only ten captive individuals. In 1991 the International Union for the Conservation of Nature urged that Mexican wolf recovery should be given priority over all other wolf conservation projects. By 1995 the total captive population of Mexican wolves had reached 136.

1980: The red wolf, *Canis rufus*, was declared extinct in the wild.

1982: A "nonessential, experimental" amendment was added to the Endangered Species Act to allow greater flexibility in the reintroduction of captive-bred or captured endangered species. The amendment placated local residents of wolf recovery areas because it allowed individuals to "take" wolves that were killing livestock on private land.

1985: Minnesota's proposal for sport harvest of wolves was rejected. Alaska authorized a statewide land-and-shoot wolf hunting policy that allowed hunters to track wolves by air, but forced them to land to kill the wolves. To shoot, they had to be at least one hundred yards from the plane. This new policy was a violation of the 1972 aerial hunting ban, and the nation protested.

1987: A five-year experiment was begun to reestablish a population of red wolves in the wild. The first four pairs of red wolves, fitted with radio telemetry devices, were released into the Alligator River National Wildlife refuge in North Carolina. At the end of five years, the program was declared a suc-

Red Wolf Recovery

The USFWS-sponsored red wolf reintroduction program, initiated in North Carolina, took a great deal of care to address the concerns of the public. Without such attention the program would not have succeeded. The following have been the keys to the success of red wolf recovery:

1. No significant restrictions were made on land use, and previous regulations remained unchanged.
2. The USFWS has worked with landowners to address their concerns.
3. Many hunters, trappers, and private landowners supported red wolf reintroduction, actively reporting sightings of red wolves.
4. The wolves have been a draw for tourists, which has resulted in an unexpected increase of local revenue.

Though it is one of the first such programs, and in many ways the most successful, the red wolf reintroduction program still suffers from funding difficulties, serious legal battles, and opposition from individuals and organizations. Without the dedication of USFWS employees, volunteers, and supporters, the program would long since have failed. This ongoing political struggle is mirrored by the difficulties that red wolves have faced: susceptibility to deadly parasites, hybridization issues with coyotes, and the continual threat of human persecution.

Symbolic of this struggle is the story of the wolf named 344F (for "female") by USFWS biologists, who assign numbers to wolves to avoid personifying them. As one of the first red wolves born wild in North Carolina in nearly two hundred years, 344F began her life dramatically: her mother died of a uterine infection when the pup was only eight weeks old, and for the next five months she was raised by her father and stepmother. When her father suffocated on a raccoon kidney, her stepmother was trapped and returned to captivity, where she was paired with a mate and eventually rereleased.

The USFWS had great difficulty trapping 344F. When she was trapped for the first time at the age of eleven months the USFWS learned why she was trapwise at such a young age: slight marks on her legs showed that she had been in and out of traps at least twice before. When 344F found traps she dug them up, chewed on them, and even urinated on them, possibly to warn other wolves. Because of the difficulty of capturing 334F, replacing her radio-collar batteries has been difficult and contact with her has been lost several times. USFWS knows that she lived in the Alligator River National Wildlife Refuge until she was twenty-two months old, when she traveled southward to find a mate. She succeeded, and had several litters with wolf 392M. Though no one knows what became of 334F, her offspring and other wolves continue to overcome the challenges of living under the influence of humans in the wild.

Canis rufus

cess and the experiment was extended to include more land and more wolves. By 1999, there were about one hundred sixty wolves in captivity and about one hundred red wolves in the wild, roaming a million acres of public and private land.

1987: Defenders of Wildlife announced a $100,000 compensation trust, which continues today. This program reimburses farmers the market value of stock that can be proven to have been killed by wolves throughout Arizona, New Mexico, central Idaho, and Yellowstone, and in expanding areas throughout which reintroduced wolves are starting to disperse. An effective way to protect populations of wolves from the backlash caused by livestock depredation, the program has maintained some degree of peace between ranchers and wolves.

1992: Red wolf reintroduction began in the Great Smoky Mountains National Park, but the wolves suffered from malnutrition, disease, parasites, and attacks by predators. Within a seven-year span, of the thirty-seven adults released in the park, twenty-six died or were recaptured when they settled beyond park boundaries. All thirty pups born to wolves in Great Smoky Mountains (except two, which were removed at a young age) died within their first year of life. Reintroduction to Great Smoky Mountains National Park was discontinued in spring 1999.

1993: According to the Convention on International Trade in Endangered Species, six thousand to seven thousand gray wolf skins have been traded annually since 1981.

1994: Two North Carolina counties suddenly passed resolutions demanding the eviction of red wolves, and in 1995 the North Carolina legislature—previously neutral—enacted a state law legalizing the killing of wolves on private property.

1995: Wolves were brought to Yellowstone National Park from Canada and were set in holding pens. USFWS used a "soft" release for these wolves: they were kept in temporary enclosures throughout the park so that they could become accustomed to the area before their release. On March 23, 1995, sixty-four years after the last Yellowstone wolves had been killed, the captive wolves were released. The wolves were able to reestablish themselves as a major predator, filling a gap in the ecosystem. In twenty-one years of planning and political struggle, the reintroduction of wolves to Yellowstone cost the government approximately six million dollars.

1995–97: Thirty-five Canadian wolves were brought to the Montana region of Yellowstone National Park and to locations in Idaho. In 1997, eleven litters were born to eight wolf packs in Yellowstone. Two of the packs allowed two litters, and one even allowed three litters, a sign that prey and territory were plentiful enough to support many pups. The wolves preyed upon elk weakened by a long winter, and it has been verified that wolves are killing bison as well. Visitors traveling Yellowstone Park's northeast road have consistently been able to glimpse wolves in the early morning and late evening. Hundreds of wolf sightings have occurred in that region in just one summer, and millions of dollars of Yellowstone tourist revenue are attributed to the addition of wolves to the park. By 1999 the shared wolf population of Yellowstone and Idaho had grown to three hundred.

1995: Alaska created the Fortymile Herd Recovery/Management Plan, which employed wolf control to increase the caribou population to pre-1920s numbers in an area between the Yukon River and the Alaska Highway, near the Canadian border. In 1997, control techniques expanded to include sterilization, relocation, and an unofficial bounty. Critics of the program claim that caribou herds are plentiful elsewhere in Alaska, and that wolf control is only being employed to keep herds at unnaturally high numbers in areas easily accessible to human hunters.

1996: The Red List, a listing of endangered species formed by the World Conservation Union, classified the wolf as vulnerable.

March 1997: The U.S. secretary of state authorized the reintroduction of the Mexican wolf in Arizona's Blue Range area. In April 1998, the long-awaited reintroduction began in the Apache Sitgraves National Forest with the release of eleven wolves.

Legal Battles

Those opposing wolf reintroduction have shown in many odd ways that they did not agree with the government's choices. The following legal battles are a select few of the struggles that took place, and in some cases continue, in the nation's courts. These lawsuits are rarely about wolves; they focus on government-imposed restrictions on what people can and cannot do on private and public land. The wolf is simply the unfortunate scapegoat.

⊹ Retaliation to the release of wolves in Yellowstone in 1995 was widespread and extreme. Idaho State Representative Bruce Newcomb announced that perhaps one way to oppose wolf reintroduction in Idaho and Yellowstone was to secede from the union. The Montana state legislature passed a resolution to introduce wolves ". . . into every other ecosystem and region of the United States, including Central Park in New York City, the Presidio in San Francisco, and Washington, D.C." The Wyoming legislature proposed a bill that would fix a five-hundred-dollar bounty on wolves and would require the state attorney general to defend any wolf killers prosecuted by the federal government.

⊹ The Montana Stock Growers filed suit to stop the second release of wolves in Yellowstone, fearing that the presence of more wolves would mean greater livestock losses. The funds for reintroduction were intentionally cut by Congress to halt wolf releases in 1996.

⊹ Alaska has been through many legal battles involving wolf control, especially the controversial land-and-shoot policy. In 1996, Alaska's citizens introduced a wildlife protection law to end land-and-shoot hunting. The law provided that aircraft could only be used to kill wolves in the case of a biological emergency. In 1999 the Alaska legislature repealed a portion of the law, removing restrictions on government hunting although independent polls showed that 70 percent of Alaska's voters opposed the repeal.

⊹ The American Farm Bureau (AFB), claiming to represent the interests of farmers, continues to file lawsuits to eliminate the protection of wolves.

Declaring that the Yellowstone Park reintroduction of wolves was illegal, the AFB filed a lawsuit. In 1997 Judge Downes, a district court judge in Wyoming, decided "with utmost reluctance" that the reintroduced wolf population and its "nonessential, experimental" designation might be detrimental to the existing wolves, which he felt might eventually repopulate the park naturally. The appeal was not heard until 1999. If the court had found in favor of the AFB, the current wolf population of Yellowstone and Idaho (some three hundred wolves) would have had to be destroyed. Fortunately, the federal appeals court in Denver reversed the lower court's ruling on January 13, 2000. Special-interest groups like the AFB (ranked seventeenth among the twenty-five most powerful special-interest groups in Washington, according to a December 1997 survey by *Fortune* magazine) are the political bane of reintroduced wolves' existence.

⊹ A lawsuit filed by the New Mexico Cattle Growers Association in 1998 claimed that reintroduced Mexican wolves were coyote or dog hybrids, and that, since there were already wolves in the Southwestern mountains, reintroduction wasn't necessary. An argument added while the lawsuit was underway maintained that Mexican wolves took food away from Mexican spotted owls, birds from which ranchers claimed to "derive substantial aesthetic enjoyment." On October 28, 1999, Judge Mechem, a senior U.S. district Judge in Albuquerque, New Mexico, ruled in favor of the wolf reintroduction program, maintaining that there was adequate scientific evidence to dismiss the case.

These legal battles are only the tip of the iceberg in the war against wolves. Animals have been shot and killed to protest reintroduction programs and government involvement. However, wolf reintroduction has moved ahead despite significant obstacles, and it is expected that in time wolf recovery will become less controversial.

In pastoral societies the wolf is commonly viewed negatively in the countryside but neutrally or positively in the city. Rural inhabitants often resent government-hired biologists who come to their communities to study wolves.

It had been more than seventeen years since this area was last populated by wolves. By the end of 1998, five of the eleven wolves had been shot and killed in separate incidents. Of the remaining six wolves (of which one was missing and presumed dead, and another was run over by a car), four were recaptured by federal biologists and returned to captivity. Locals' Old West–antigovernment attitude has been voiced via the shooting of wolves and threats to U.S. Forest Service employees.

March 1999: Three more Mexican wolves were reintroduced to the Apache Sitgraves National Forest. By the following summer, nineteen more wolves had been released.

Spring 1999: One wolf traveled to Oregon from Idaho, traversing 150 miles of ranches, rivers, and interstate highways. This journey, which made her the first wolf in Oregon in thirty-six years, illustrates a wolf's persistence when seeking new territory.

Late 1999: Approximately two hundred Mexican wolves were known to exist in captivity and about twenty-four wolves (four packs) survived in the wild.

Winter 1999: The European Action Plan for Large Carnivores was approved. The European Union will base much of its funding for individual countries on this plan. Such plans are vital to the wolf populations of European countries, since the animal does not know political borders. For example, France has been considering what to do with its population of forty wolves; if the French are unwilling to put up with such a small number, it brings into question why Romania should have to deal with its 2,500 wolves. In addition, poaching issues in western Poland affect the natural repopulation of wolves into Germany from that country.

In the U.S., scientists have been studying wolves for the past sixty years. Research money has been allotted to understanding the animals in order to manage them better. American and Canadian research has far exceeded that of any other country in funding; Mongolia, for example, is relying on information gathered in the mid–1980s, since little current data are available. Such countries don't know enough about their wolf populations to manage them. In Portugal, bad wildlife management is considered to be the worst threat to wolves.

In some cases, it is more beneficial for the wolf to be considered a game species for the sake of funding research. Kazakhstan has recently reclassified the wolf from "noxious animal" to game animal, creating a positive attitude toward the animal and a more controlled management, as opposed to uncontrolled poaching. In Romania, the cost of having wolves is equal to the money earned through ecotourism. (Each wolf is projected to cost farmers $600 per year for livestock loss/compensation and in the expenses of taking preventive measures against further depredation.) With the increasing revenues of ecotourism, the hope is that the attitude towards wolves will be more positive. Interest in wolves is increasing in most countries, and the resulting upswing in research and education is greatly beneficial to them.

Defending Wolves

In the wake of wolf reintroduction and repopulation, affording protection to wild wolves is one of the best ways to secure the wolf's survival. The following ideas are currently employed or suggested by biologists:

- Develop more research, secure additional funding, and establish a worldwide information exchange.
- Set up a compensation fund to cover livestock lost to wolves (a technique proven effective by the Defenders of Wildlife program), and recommend methods to cut losses.
- Wrap fluorescent tape around wolves' radio collars, or spray reintroduced wolves with fluorescent paint in order to distinguish them from other canids.

- In countries where wolf hunting is legal, provide seven-mile buffer zones that prohibit hunting around wildlife parks.
- Establish protected no-kill wildlife corridors to provide wolves with access to other parks to reduce genetic isolation and/or gene swamping by coyotes.
- Temporarily forbid logging and other heavy land use for a 1.5- to 9-mile radius around denning sites. This will keep adults from being obstructed when bringing food to the den, and will protect the pups from being moved too early by adult wolves made nervous by humans.
- Enforce laws intended to protect wolves.
- Encourage faithful and honest depictions, not stereotypes, in publications and films about wolves.

Romanticizing the Wolf

Recently, tourists have flooded the few national parks in which wolves live in the hope of seeing, or just hearing, the animal. Two thousand people have been known to attend a single evening of regularly scheduled wolf howls at Algonquin National Park, Canada. Even parks without wolf populations attract enormous attention—and often a larger audience than they expect—when they invite speakers who bring their captive wolves. In Yellowstone National Park, wolves have been disrupted from vital activities such as bringing food to their pups. The presence of humans near den sites can also force the wolf pack to move pups from the birth den too early. Wolves become tense and uneasy in close contact with humans.

Surviving

Habitat destruction and the campaign against wolves have led to near extinction of the wolf throughout most of Europe, Asia, and the lower forty-eight United States. In the aftermath of their persecution, various subspecies of the gray wolf have been declared extinct in the wild; the Mexican and red wolf exist only in captivity and in experimental populations in the wild; and the Ethiopian wolf is critically endangered. Humans have killed at least one million wolves in the United States alone. Despite seemingly insurmountable losses, the wolf has managed to survive. Approximately two hundred thousand wolves—once the population of the Great Plains region alone—currently reside in fifty-seven countries.

- Wolves have survived, though they are threatened to varying degrees, in Canada, Alaska, Russia, and China.
- Though enormously reduced in population, wolves have also survived in the Near and Middle East, northern India, northern Spain, Eastern Europe, and the Italian Apennines Mountains.
- Strong wolf populations currently exist in Minnesota, Idaho, Montana, Wisconsin, and Michigan.
- Small but growing wolf populations are reestablishing themselves in Wyoming, Washington, Germany, France, Finland, Norway, and Sweden.
- Sightings of wolves have been reported in Maine and Oregon.
- Wolves have been reintroduced into Yellowstone, North Carolina, and New Mexico.

- Restoration of wolves is also being planned for the North Woods (New Hampshire, New York, Maine, Vermont), Olympic Park (Washington State), Arizona, California, Colorado, Oregon, Scotland, and Japan.

Public perception of the wolf is shifting, and we are slowly beginning to understand and respect this maligned animal. Ecologically, the time is ripe for wolves to return to the habitats that can still sustain them. Wolves regulate the prey population and as a result guard the land from being overgrazed; environments that once supported the wolf are healthier when wolves are present. In addition to their role in the natural order, wolves also serve as a political umbrella species. The preservation of their expansive habitat benefits equally endangered but less prominent species.

Although the ecological need for wolves is clear, the issue of reintroducing them into their former habitat is complex. The costs of reintroduction are both financial and ethical: under current reintroduction and management programs, wolves are heavily monitored, and are killed when humans deem it necessary. Is a heavily managed wolf still a wild wolf?

Our ignorance and intolerance are still the primary threats to the wolf's existence. When our ancestors saw eyes glowing in the flicker of firelight, or shadows weaving in and out of the dark forest, they felt admiration, fear, respect, and awe. Once gone, the wolf cannot be replaced. Open your eyes, your mind, and your heart. We still have much to learn from the wolf.

NOTES, SECTION 3

1. Christine Mlot, "Stalking the Ancient Dog," *Science News* 151 (June 28, 1997), 400-01.

2. W. Francis H. King, *Classical and Foreign Quotations* (New York: Frederick Unger Publishing Co. 1965), #935.

3. Steven H. Fritts, et al., *Trends and Management of Wolf-Livestock Conflicts in Minnesota*, Resource Publication 181 (Washington, D.C.: U.S. Fish and Wildlife Service, 1992).

4. Charles Bergman, "Spain's Wolf Wars," *International Wildlife* (March-April 1997): 22-29.

5. Rick Bass, *The Ninemile Wolves* (Livingstone, Montana: Clark City Press, 1992), 71.

6. Arcturos (civil society for the protection and management of wildlife and the natural environment), "Conservation of Canis lupus in central Greece," unpublished results of the LIFE NAT 4249 project.

7. Snorri Sturlasson, *Heimskringla* (trans. Samuel Laing 1844 www.sunsite.berkeley.edu/OMACL/Heimskringla). A history of Scandinavian kings and collection of poems compiled in A.D. 1225.

8. St. Jerome, Letter LXVIII to Castrius (Christian Classics Ethereal Library, Calvin College, www.wheaton.edu/fathers/NPNF2-06/letters/letter68.htm).

9. Bruce Hampton, *The Great American Wolf* (New York: Henry Holt and Company, Inc., 1997).

10. Snorri Sturlasson, *Heimskringla*.

11. Unknown, Annalist of Neider-Altaich, "The Great German Pilgrimage of 1064-65", (trans. James Brundage, Medieval Sourcebook: www.fordham.edu/halsall/source/1064pilgrim.html). Paragraph #9.

12. Bruce Hampton, *The Great American Wolf*, 87.

13. Richard I. Dodge, *The Hunting Grounds of the Great West* (London: Chatto and Windus, 1878).

14. Bertil Hagalund, *Järv och Varg* (Stockholm, 1965).

15. Vilhjelmer Stefansson, *Adventures in Error* (New York: Robert M. McBride, 1936).

16. David L. Mech, *The Wolf: The Ecology and Behavior of an Endangered Species* (New York: American Museum of Natural History, 1970), 293.

17. Adolph Murie, *The Wolves of Mt. McKinley* (Washington: University of Washington Press, 1987), 22.

18. Newfoundland Museum (www.nfmuseum.com/notes8.html).

19. William Hornaday, *The American Natural History* (New York: Charles Scribner's Sons, 1904).

20. Murie, *The Wolves of Mt. McKinley*, 230-31.

21. Ernest Thompson Seton, *Lobo, King of the Currumpaw*, 1894.

22. John Theberge and Mary Theberge, *Wolf Country: Eleven Years Tracking the Algonquin Wolves* (Toronto, Ontario: McClelland & Stewart, Inc., 1998), 178-92.

23. Jonathan Waterman, "Sheep's Clothing: Alaskan Wolf Control: Is It Wildlife Biology? Or Plain Old Politics?" *Outside Magazine* (May 93): 51-60.

Index

A

Aberdeen Bestiary, 81, 94
Abydos, 85
Acadia, 68
Adaptability, 28–29
Aerial hunting, 115, 120, 121, 124
Affectionate behavior, 9
Africa, 101, 103
Afterlife, 84
Aggression, 26, 35, 38–41, 113
Ahriman, 79, 103
Ainu, 71
Alarm, 35
Alaska, 115, 120, 121, 123, 124, 128
Algonquin National Park, 9, 16, 28, 44,
    113, 121, 127
Alligator River National Wildlife Refuge,
    121–23
Alpha wolves, 4, 6, 8, 23, 24–25, 26, 31,
    45
Amala, 89
Amber, 77
American Farm Bureau (AFB), 124
Anamaqkin, 79
Anatomy, 18–19, 44
Annalist of Nieder-Altaich, 108
Anubis, 85
Apache Sitgraves National Forest, 123,
    126
Apennines Mountains, 128
Apocalypse, 76
Apollo, 74, 76, 79, 83
Appalachian Mountains, 110
Arctic Wild (Crisler), 53
Arctic wolf, 14, 29
Ares, 68
Argus, 83
Aristotle, 57
Arizona, 123, 126, 128
Artemis, 70
Artwork, 58–59
Asia, 15, 76, 128. See also China; Mongolia
Asvins, 82
Atet barque, 84
Athens, Greece, 103
Attacks, 98, 104–6, 109, 112, 113, 115.
    See also livestock
Attention, 35
Avesta, 77

B

Baglioni family, 96
Bailey, Vernon, 119
Baltic mythology, 74, 77
Barking, 35
Baronius, Caesar, 106
Baths, 28
Beast of Gévaudan, 112–13
Behavior, 2

Bering land bridge, 17, 101, 103
Berserkers, 64
Bessi, 87
Beta wolves, 6, 23, 25
Biblical references, 79, 81, 90–93, 103, 109
Birth, 5–6, 94
Bison, 110, 111, 114
Blackfoot, 63, 76
Blanca, 117
Blue-gray wolf, 107
Blue Range area, 123
Body language, 8, 38–39
Bounties, 103–6, 110, 114–16, 120, 123,
    124
Bowman, Elbert, 118
Brandenburg, Jim, 28
Breeding. See Mating
Budge, E. A. Wallis, 85
Buffalo wolf, 14, 101
Bukhari, 71
Byzantine symbolism, 82

C

Caching, 28
California, 128
Canada, 79, 110, 120, 123, 126, 128
Canidae line, 101
Canis familiaris, 19
Canis lupaster, 84
Canis lupus. See Gray wolf
Canis lupus albus, 15
Canis lupus arctos, 14, 29
Canis lupus baileyi. See Mexican wolf
Canis lupus campestris, 15
Canis lupus familiaris. See Dogs, domestic
Canis lupus hattai, 15
Canis lupus hodophiliax, 15
Canis lupus laniger, 15
Canis lupus lupus, 15
Canis lupus lycaon, 14, 75, 111
Canis lupus nubilus, 14, 101
Canis lupus occidentalis, 14
Canis lupus pallipes, 15, 114
Canis rufus. See Red wolf
Canis simensis, 5, 17, 128
Canute, King of England, 86
Cape Cod, Mass., 110
Captive wolves, 11, 20–21, 25, 126, 128
Caribou, 123
Cattle. See Livestock
Celts, 62, 76, 77
Central Asian Steppes, 76
Cerberus, 82
Cerennunos, 70
Ceres, 62
Charon, 79
Cheyenne, 63, 79
Children, 89, 108, 112
China, 15, 102, 120, 128

Christianity, 90–93, 103
Christmastide, 81
Cicero, Marcus Tullius, 57
Ciliades, 103
Civilization, 96, 100, 103, 121
Ciziges, 87
Clans, wolf, 66–69
Cleanliness, 28
Coins, 76, 86
Colonists, 109–10
Colorado, 124, 128
Common wolf, 15
Communication, 113.
    See also Body language; Vocalization
Constellations, 74, 76
Convention on International Trade in
    Endangered Species, 123
Coralli, 87
Cormac Airt, 68
Coyotes, 16, 18–19, 50, 101, 109, 110,
    115, 120, 124, 127
Crater Lake National Park, 111
Crime. see Outlaws, wolves as
Crisler, Lois, 20, 30, 53
Cro-Magnon paintings, 67
Cruelty toward wolves, 117–19
Curran, James, 115
Currumpaw Valley, N. Mex., 116

D

Dakota, 83
Dark Ages, 96
Death, 8, 9–11, 78–79, 82, 84
Deer, 110, 115
Defenders of Wildlife, 123, 127
Demeter, temple of, 62
Denali National Park, 111, 115
Denmark, 87
Denning, 4
Denver, Colo., 124
Depredation, 104–5, 109–10.
    See also Livestock
Devils, 80–81, 90, 93, 94, 97, 103, 106,
    109
Diffidentia, 103
Dionysus, 68
Dis Pater, 86
Dispersers, 8, 11, 17, 54, 105
Dodge, Richard Irving, 112
Dog-wolf. See Wolf-dog hybrid
Dogs, 82; domestic, 15, 18–19, 102–4,
    110; wild, 104
Dolan, 67
Domestication, 102, 103
Dominance, 4, 7, 23, 24, 35, 38, 45.
    See also Alpha wolves
Downes, Judge, 124
Droma, 65
Dusk, 76, 77. See also Night

E

Eastern timber wolf, 14, 75, 111
Eclipses, 76
Ecosystem, 50–51, 72, 123, 128
Ecotourism, 126. *See also* Hunting, sport
Edgar, King of England, 106
Edward the Confessor, 86, 106
Egypt, 83
Egyptians, 62, 79, 82, 84–85, 93, 103
Ellesmere Island, 44
Endangered species, 120, 121, 123
England, 107
Eradication, 105–8, 110, 111, 115,
    117–19, 120, 124
Ethiopian wolf, 5, 17, 128
Etruscan paintings, 78, 79
Eurasia, 101, 103
Euripides, 67
Europe, 15, 79, 81–83, 87, 88, 93, 101,
    107, 108, 112, 120, 126, 128
European Action Plan for Large Carnivores,
    126
European Union, 126
Extinct species, 14, 15, 84, 121, 128
Ezo wolf of Hokkaido, 15

F

Fables, 103, 107–8, 112
Faunus, 60, 70
Fear, 112, 113
Fence, 110
Fenris, 64–65, 83
Fertility, 60–62, 70, 103
Fights, 24, 25
Finland, 128
Finno-Ugrians, 79
Fire, 118
Florida, 16
Folklore, 94–95, 111, 112.
    See also Fables; Mythology
Font de Gaume cave, 102
Food, 7–9, 22, 28, 42–49, 102, 111, 114
Fortymile Herd Recovery/Management
    Plan, 123
Foxes, 101, 109
France, 79, 81, 87, 88, 90, 100, 102, 103,
    105, 107, 112–13, 126, 128
Franks, laws of, 86
Freki, 62, 83
Frontiersmen, 110–11
Fuente, Felix Rodriguez de la, 121
Fuga, 70
Fur, 28–29
Fylgia, 62

G

Gallows, 86
Garnier, Gilles, 88, 89
Genghis Khan, 107
Geri, 62, 83
German, Old High, 62
Germany, 76, 81–83, 87, 126, 128
Getae, 87
Gévaudan, France, 112–13

Gillham, Arkansas, 119
Girgentis, 67
Glacier National Park, 111
Gleipner, 65
Goats, 60, 82
Gobin, R., 91
Godamuri, India, 89
Grain, 83
Grain wolf, 60
Grand battues, 106
Grand Canyon National Park, 111
Grass wolf, 60
Gray wolf, 12–16, 28, 101, 123, 128
"The Great German Pilgrimage of 1064-
    1065," 108
Great Lakes region, 110
Great Plains, 110–11, 114, 128
Great Plains wolf, 14, 101
Great Smoky Mountains National Park,
    123
Greece, 62, 68, 70, 74, 79, 82, 83, 86, 93,
    103, 105
Green wolf, 60
Growling, 35
Gundestrup Cauldron, 70

H

Hades, 78, 82
Hafnersfjord, battle at, 106
"The Hammer of Witches," 106
Hati, 76
Hatred of wolves, 87, 90–91, 93–95, 98,
    100, 103, 105, 109, 115, 117–19
Hebrew legend, 93
Hecate, 79
Henry I, King of France, 86
Herodotus, 62, 68
Hierarchy system. *See* Social structure
Highwaymen, 86
Hinduism, 82, 83
Hirpi Sorani, 86
A Historie of Foure-Footed Beastes (Topsell),
    82, 94–95
History: chronology, 98–126
Hornady, William, 115
Hornklofe, 106, 107
Howling, 2, 7, 32, 36–37, 52, 72, 81, 83,
    93. *See also* Vocalization
Hrafnsmál, 68
Humans, 58–69, 101; attitudes toward
    wolves, 96, 100, 103, 105, 115–20,
    126–28; illness in, 71; wolf deaths
    and, 9, 11; wolf-like, 32, 66–69,
    86–91, 103; wolves as spiritual leaders
    and teachers of, 62–63, 72; wolves'
    avoidance of, 112, 113, 127.
    See also Colonists; Hatred of wolves;
    History; Respect for wolves; Vikings;
    Werewolves
Hunthr etha vargr vidar, 83
Hunting, 7, 42, 47–48, 110; regulation of,
    127; sport, 111, 115, 121, 123, 126;
    wolves assisting humans, 63, 101, 103;
    of wolves by humans, 110–11,
    114–18, 124. *See also* Bounties

I

Iazyges, 87
Idaho, 123, 124, 126, 128
Illness, 25, 71, 89
In Praise of Wolves (Lawrence), 5, 53
India, 67, 89, 117, 128
Inquisition, 88
Instinct, 40
International Union for the Conservation
    of Nature, 121
Inuit, 63, 72, 79
Iran, 67, 83, 103
Ireland, 68, 108
Islam, 67
Isle Royale, Mich., 28
Italy, 62, 67, 70, 87, 96, 120, 128

J

Jackals, 17, 85, 101
James I, King of England, 88
Japan, 60, 63, 71, 128
Judgement Day, 79
Justice, 25

K

Kamala, 89
Kaput, 83
Kazakhstan, 126
Kennedy, W. R., 115
Khanukh, 83
Khenti Amenti. *See* Upuaut
Kirgis, 76
Kwakiutl, 72, 73

L

Laeding, 65
Land-and-shoot hunting policy.
    See Aerial hunting
Land use, 127
Lascoweic, 70
Latvian folklore, 81
Lawrence, R. D., 5, 31, 53
Lawsuits, 124
Legends. *See* Fables; Folklore; Mythology
Legislation, 110, 114, 115, 120, 121, 123,
    124, 127
Leshii, 70
Leto, 74, 83
Levant, 103
Lewis, Meriwether, 70
*Life of Anskar, the Apostle of the North,
    801-865* (Rimbert), 96
Lin Piao, 120
Linné, Carl, 108
Lisun, 93
Litter size, 5
"Little Red Riding Hood" (Perrault), 107
Livestock, 61, 103–5, 109–10, 114–16,
    118, 123, 124, 126, 127
Lobo, 116–17
Lok, 76
Loki, 65
Lone wolves. *See* Dispersers
Long Island, N.Y., 118

Loophole, 87
Lopez, Barry, 20, 94
Loping, 19
Loreto, holy house of, 106
Loup hole, 87
Louvre museum, 107
Lower-ranking wolves, 6, 23, 25
Luke, 74
Lukogenes, 74
Lukoi, 68
Lukos, 74
Lupercalia, 60
Lycanthropy, 75, 88, 107.
    See also Werewolves
Lycaon, 75
Lycastus, 68
Lycopolis, 74, 85

M

Mackenzie Valley wolf, 14
Macrobius, 74, 82
Maenads, 68
Maine, 128
Mainz, archbishop of, 107
Mairya, 68
Males, 4
Malleus Maleficarum, 106
Management, 115–24, 126–28.
    See also Eradication
Managram, 76
Mange, 115, 118
Mani, 76
Manifesto of Wolf Conservation, 120
Männerbund, 68
Maria, Francesco, 106
Mars, 61, 70, 79
Masks, 67, 68, 71–73
Massachusetts, 110
Masters of the wolf, 70
Mating, 4, 8, 17, 22, 24, 38, 39, 120, 121
Mayalde, Count of Spain, 121
Mazda-Zoroaster worshippers, 77
Mech, David, 20, 21, 28, 53, 113
Mechem, Judge, 124
Menominee, 79
Mesa Verde National Park, 111
Mexican wolf, 14, 121, 123, 125, 126, 128
Michigan, 28, 121, 128
Middle Ages, 90, 94, 108
Middle East, 102, 128
Milky Way, 76
Minnesota, 104, 121, 128
Mississippi Valley, 110
Mongolia, 67, 126
Montana, 104, 114, 115, 123, 124, 128
Montana Stock Growers, 124
Monuments. *See* Sculpture
Moon, 76, 77, 94
Moqwaio, 79
Morality, 100, 103, 106
Morocco, 68
Mount Rainier National Park, 111
Mourning, 11
Mt. McKinley/Denali National Park, 111, 115
Muir, John, 63

Murie, Adolph, 5, 94, 113, 115
Mythology, 56–89, 98, 112; afterlife, 84;
    Ainu, 71; change and destruction,
    76–77; fertility, 60–61; leadership,
    62–63; magic of the wolf, 66–68; mas-
    ters of the wolf, 70; New World, 109;
    outlaw, 86–87; passage of time, 82;
    strength, 64–67; werewolf transforma-
    tion, 75; witches and devils, 80–81.
    See also Fables; Folklore

N

Narmer palette, 85
Naskapi Cree, 79
Native Americans, 62, 63, 66, 72, 73, 79,
    102. *See also specific tribes*
Navajo, 81
Near East, 128
Nebraska, 79
Neuri, 68
New Hampshire, 128
New Mexico, 116, 123, 124, 128
New World, 109–10
New York, 110, 128
Newcomb, Bruce, 124
Newfoundland wolf, 115
Newspapers, 115
Night, 76, 77, 82, 83
Ninemile Valley, Mont., 104
No-kill wildlife corridors, 127
Normandy, France, 79, 86
North America, 14, 98, 101, 103, 109–11
North Carolina, 110, 121–23, 128
North Woods, 128
Northern Michigan University, 121
Norway, 62, 74, 128

O

Oddi family, 96
Odin, 62, 64–65, 79, 83
Of Wolves and Men (Lopez), 94
Oglala Sioux, 63
Okuchi-no-kami, 60
Old age, 8, 95
Old Norse, 62–63, 76, 87
Olympic Park, 128
Omaha tribe, 79
Omega wolves, 6, 23, 25
Onega, Lake, 67
Oneida, 73
Opoïs Wepwawet. *See* Upuaut
Opprobrium lupula, 81
Oregon, 126, 128
Osiris, 84, 85
Outlaws, wolves as, 86–87, 106, 112,
    116–17
Ovid, 87

P

Packs, 4, 6, 8, 22–26, 36, 58, 104, 117.
    See also Social structure
Paleo-Indians, 103
Parks, national, 50, 111, 115, 123,
    124, 127, 128. *See also* Algonquin
    National Park

Parrhasius, 68
Parricide, 87
Passion, 40–41
Pawnee, 76
Paws, 19
Pea wolf, 60
Peltage, 15, 110, 111, 123
Perrault, Charles, 107
Persia, 79. *See also* Iran
Perugia, Italy, 96
Petroglyphs, 66, 101
Pets. *See* Captive wolves
Phaedo (Plato), 88
Phoebus Apollo. *See* Apollo
Plague, 107
Plato, 88, 94
Play, 6, 30–31, 38
Pliny, 57
Pluto, 86
Plymouth Rock, 109
Poaching, 126. *See also* Hunting
Poetry, 73, 76, 83
Poison, 111, 115–17, 119
Poland, 126
Politics, 121
Population, 50–51, 70, 114, 118, 120, 126,
    128. *See also* Management
Portugal, 126
Predatory Animal and Rodent Control
    service (PARC), 118
Prey. *See* Food
Pro Caelio (Cicero), 57
Prose Edda, 76, 83
Punishment, wolves sent as, 106
Pups, 4–7, 32, 104, 113

R

Rabies, 111, 112, 115, 120
Raudfeldson, Thorleif, 64
"Raven Song" (Hornklofe), 107
Ravening Wolves (Gobin), 91
Ravens, 52–53, 63, 72
Red List, 123
Red wolf, 14, 16, 42, 72, 101, 119–23, 128
Reindeer, 115
Reintroduction programs, 121–28.
    See also Population
Religion, 90–94, 103, 106.
    See also Biblical references; Spirituality
Rendezvous sites, 7. *See also* Territory
Research, 21, 113, 114, 121, 126, 127
Respect for wolves, 73, 87, 93
Rimbert, Bishop, 96
Rocky Mountain National Park, 111
Roman sculpture, 85
Romania, 78, 126
Rome, Italy, 62, 67, 87.
    See also Romulus and Remus
Romulus and Remus, 61, 102, 103.
    See also Rome, Italy
Rural environments, 120
Russia, 68, 70, 81, 87, 112, 120, 128
Rutu, 79

S

Saami, 68, 70, 79, 87, 100, 118
Sabbaths, 81
St. Andrew's Feast, 70, 93
St.-Anne-la-Palud, 63
St. Christopher, 93
St. Edumnd, 93
St. Francis, 93
St. George, 70, 92, 93
St. Hervé, 63, 93
St. Jerome, 107
St. Maedoc, 93
St. Nicholas, 70
St. Peter, 93
Saints, 93
Sanskrit, 62
Sarmatians, 87
Saudi Arabia, 118
Sault Ste. Marie *Daily Star*, 115
Savage, 96
Scandinavia, 64, 67, 68
Scavengers, 44, 50, 51, 58, 104, 107, 110
Scent marking, 26–27
Science, 94–95, 106
Scotland, 87, 108, 128
Scotland-Ardross, 60
Sculpture, 62, 85
Scythians, 87
Seasons, 82. *See also* Winter
Sekhemtaui, 85
Sektet barque, 84–85
Sequoia National Park, 111
Serapis, 82
Serbian word for wolf, 62, 87
Set guns, 118
Seton, Ernest Thompson, 115–17, 119
"The Seven Little Goats [or Geese]", 82,
    107
Shamans, 67, 68
Sheepdogs, 105
Shepherds, 105, 113
Shinto, 60
Shrines, 60
Siberia, 76, 79
Sicilians, 67
Silva, 96
Sin, 90–91
Singh, Reverend, 89
Sitting Bull, 62
Skáldskaparmál (Sturlasson), 83
Skoll, 76
Slavic wolf spirits, 70, 76, 83
Smithsonian Institution, 19
Snow, 54. *See also* Winter
Snowshoes, 63
Social structure, 6–7, 11, 22–25, 36, 38, 58
Socrate, 86
Sol, 76
Soranus, 86
Spain, 104, 120, 128
Special interest groups, 121
Spirituality, 62–63, 71–72. *See also* Religion
Stalking, 3
Stephanos, Archdeacon, 93

Steppe wolf, 15
Sterilization, 123
Stockholm, Sweden, 121
Storms, 77, 83
Stubb, Peter, 107
Sturlasson, Snorri, 83
Styx, river, 79
Submission, 8, 24, 38–39, 45, 113
Subspecies, 15
Sun, 74, 76, 77, 82, 83, 84–85
Survival, 28–29
Sweden, 8, 54, 66, 83, 87, 104, 108, 121, 128
Swimming, 82

T

Tahltan, 63
Tails, 19, 39
Tanama River region, 9
Teachers, wolves as, 62–63
*The Teaching of the Lord to the Gentiles
    by the Twelve Apostles*, 89
Teeth, 44
Temperaments, 4
Territory, 7, 26–27, 47, 58
Teutonic mythology, 62, 64–65, 76, 79, 83
Theberge, John, 9, 121
Thieves, 87
"The Three Little Pigs," 83, 107
344F, 122
Tibetan wolf, 15
Time, 82
Timidity, 112, 113, 127
Timor, 70
Tlingit, 63, 83
Tonkawa, 67
Topsell, Edward, 82, 94–95
Tornados, 79
Totem animals, 62–64, 67, 68
Towq, 63
Tracks, 19
Trails, 54
Traps, 117, 122
Traveling, 7, 36, 54
Tundra wolf, 15
Tura, 67
Turkey, 67
Tyr, 65

U

Ulfhota, 68
Ulvhethnar, 64
United States, 104–5, 110–11,
    114–16, 118, 120, 124, 126, 128.
    See also specific states
United States Endangered Species Act, 120,
    121
United States Fish and Wildlife Service
    (USFWS), 104, 115, 121–22, 123
Upuaut, 62, 79, 84–85
Urban environments, 120
Urination, 26
Ursa Major, 74, 76
USFWS. *See* United States Fish and
    Wildlife Service (USFWS)

V

Valentines Day, 60
Valkyries, 79
Valhalla, 79
Vampires, 78
VanBallenberge, Vic, 121
Vancouver Island, 72
Vargamor, 81
Vargatreo, 86
Vedas, 83
Vermont, 128
Veterinarians, 115
Vikings, 64–65, 79, 83
Vila, 83
Vircolac, 76
Vision, 8, 48–49, 95
Vocalization, 19, 32, 33–34, 35–36, 94.
    See also Howling
Volsunga, 68, 79

W

Wales, King of, 106
War gods, 85
Warriors, 64, 67, 68
Washington (state), 128
Wayne, Robert, 102
Weather, 28–29, 83.
    See also Snow; Storms; Tornados
Werewolves, 68, 75, 76, 81, 86–88, 106,
    107
Westward expansion, 110–11, 114–15
Whelping. *See* Birth
"Wide-Eyed Wolf," 62
Wind, 83
Wind Cave National Park, 111
Winter, 76, 82, 85. *See also* Snow
Wisconsin, 128
Witches, 80–81
Wolf, significance of word, 62–63, 87
Wolf-dog hybrid, 19, 20, 112–13, 124
The Wolf (Mech), 53
Wolf of Honshu, 15
Wolf of India and Iraq, 15, 114
Wolf of Southern Arabia, 14, 15
"Wolf Road," 76
The Wolves of Mt. McKinley (Murie), 5, 94,
    113
World Conservation Union, 123
World War I, 115
World War II, 120
Wyoming, 111, 114, 124, 128

Y

Yakut, 76
Yellowstone National Park, 50, 111, 123,
    124, 127, 128
Yosemite National Park, 111
Young, Stanley, 111
Yupiaq, 72

Z

Zeus, 68, 75
Zion National Park, 111
Zoroastrianism, 68, 77, 79, 103

Now the house is dark again, and the corners are filled with dust and shadows. Sometimes I lie awake at night and remember. My parents say good riddance to bad waves and I am never to bring home another. But I miss my friend.

Maybe next year, if we go to the mountains, I'll bring home a cloud. Clouds are soft and cuddly and would never act like a wave.

When we returned, we found the wave frozen—a beautiful statue of ice. Though it broke my heart, I helped my father wrap her in a quilt, and we carried her back to the sea.

My father said she would have to go. My poor mother was nearly crazy. Since I could never catch the wave, we packed and went away for a time, leaving her behind in the cold.

Finally I grew angry. Now the wave spent all her time playing with the fish and never played with me. I tried to catch them, but they darted like ghosts between my fingers while the wave poured over me in foaming laughter.

With the coming of winter, the sky turned gray and the city shivered, drenched in a frozen rain. The wave had nightmares. She dreamed strange dreams of the icy regions of the poles, of turning to ice and sailing away to where the nights go on for years. She curled herself into a corner and howled through long, long days and longer nights. She filled the house with phantoms and called up monsters from the deep....

She was pulled by the moon, the sun, and the stars: Her moods were as changeable as the tide.

I thought she might be lonely and gave her seashells and a tiny sailboat to play with. After she smashed these against the wall, I brought home small fish for her. She swept them into her arms, then whispered and played with them by the hour. At night, while she slept, the fish adorned her hair with little flashes and splashes of color.

At night we lay side by side, whispering secrets with smiles and smothered laughter. She rocked me to sleep in her waters and sang sweet sea songs into the shell of my ear. Sometimes in the dark she shimmered like a rainbow. To touch her then was like touching a piece of night tattooed with fire.

Other nights she was black and bitter. In dark despair she howled and sighed and twisted. Hearing her, the sea wind came flying over the mountains. It wailed with a wild wind voice through the trees and clawed all night at my windows.

Cloudy days enraged the wave. She smashed my model train, soaked my stamp collection, and covered my room in her gray and greenish foam....

The wave and I played together constantly. If I caught and hugged her, she would rise up tall like a liquid tree, then burst into a shower and bathe me in her foam. If I ran at her and she stood still, I would find myself wrapped in her arms. She would lift me up, then let me fall, only to catch me and lower me to the floor as gently as a feather.

Before, she had been one wave; now, she was many. She flooded our rooms with light and air, driving away the shadows with her blue and green reflections. Small forgotten corners crowded with dust and dark were swept by her light. The whole house shone with her laughter. Her smile was everywhere.

The sun came into our old, dark rooms and stayed for hours and hours. It loved dancing with the wave and me so much that it sometimes forgot to leave. More than once it crept out through my window as the stars watched in amazement.

The next morning we went to the station and boarded the train. The wave was tall and fair and full of light—she was bound to attract attention. If there was a rule forbidding waves from traveling by train, the conductor might throw her off. So, cup by small cup, when no one was looking, I emptied the watercooler, and she hid herself inside it.

When we arrived home, the wave rushed into our house....

My father tried to send her back, but
the wave cried and begged and threatened
until he agreed that she could come along.

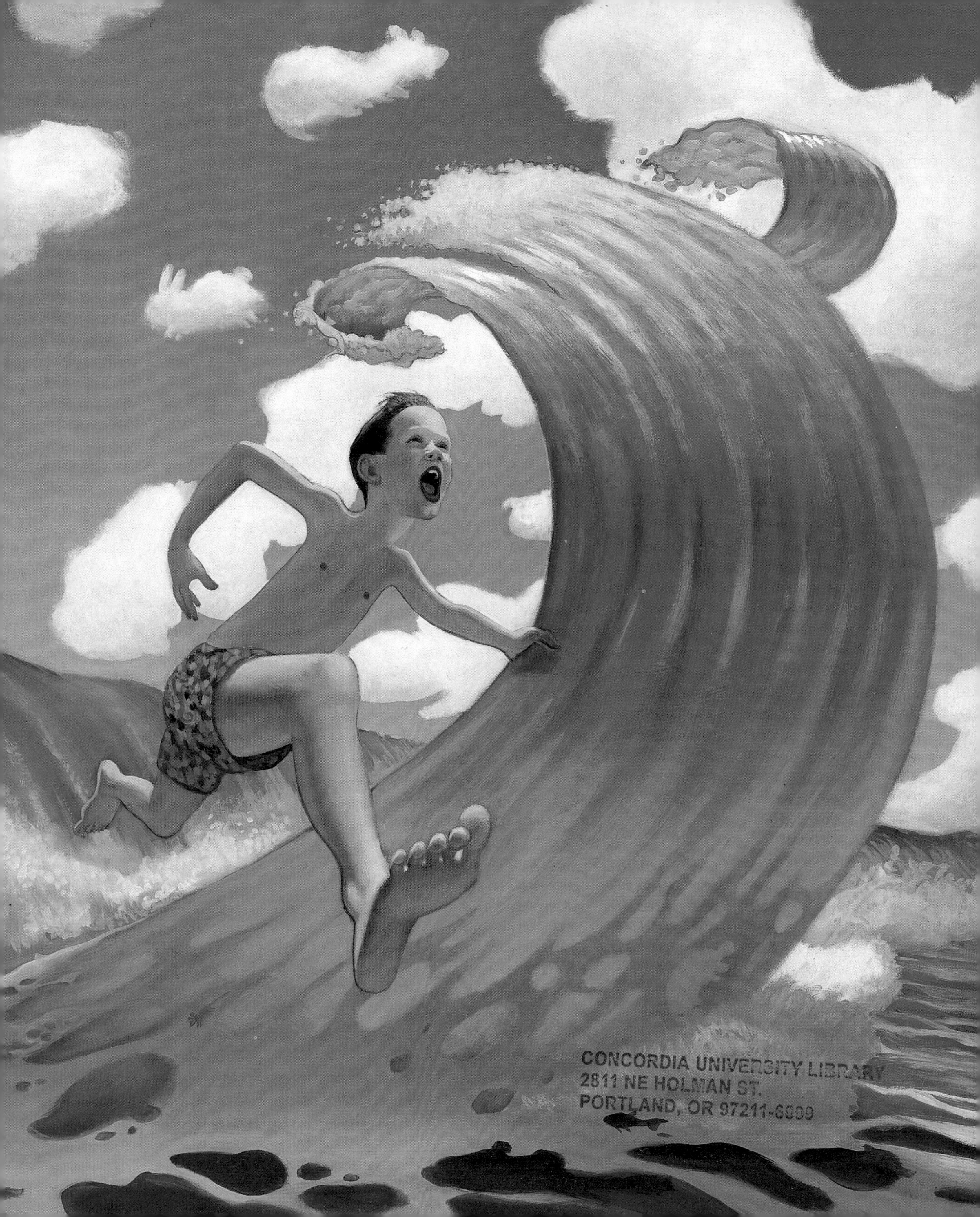

My first trip to the seashore, I fell in love with the waves. Just as we were about to leave, one wave tore away from the sea. When the others tried to stop her by clutching at her floating skirts, she caught my hand, and we raced away together across the wrinkled sand.

My Life with the Wave

Based on the story by
OCTAVIO PAZ

Translated and adapted for children by
CATHERINE COWAN

Illustrated by
MARK BUEHNER

Lothrop, Lee & Shepard Books · Morrow   New York

to Judit Bodnar
— CC

to the Gish family,
with special thanks to Carol and Griffin
— MB

This story is based on "My Life with the Wave," included in *Eagle or Sun? (¿Aguila o sol?)*, published by
New Directions Publishing Corporation. Used by permission.
Copyright © 1960 by Fondo de Cultura Economica.

Acrylic and oil paints were used for the full-color illustrations. The text type is 16-point Fenice.

Text copyright © 1997 by Catherine Cowan
Illustrations copyright © 1997 by Mark Buehner

Published by Lothrop, Lee & Shepard Books
an imprint of Morrow Junior Books
a division of William Morrow and Company, Inc.
1350 Avenue of the Americas, New York, NY 10019

Printed in the United States of America.

3 4 5 6 7 8 9 10

Library of Congress Cataloging-in-Publication Data
Cowan, Catherine. My life with the wave/by Octavio Paz; as retold for children by Catherine Cowan;
illustrated by Mark Buehner.
p. cm.
Summary: A child befriends a wave at the seashore and brings her home.
ISBN 0-688-12660-X (trade)—ISBN 0-688-12661-8 (library)
[1. Ocean waves—Fiction. 2. Friendship—Fiction.] I. Paz, Octavio. II. Buehner, Mark, ill. III. Title.
PZ7.C8347My 1994 [Fic]—dc20 93-33625 CIP AC

My Life with the Wave